MORE BOOKS BY
DAISY PRESCOTT

Love with Altitude:
Next to You
Crazy Over You
Wild for You
Up to You

Modern Love Stories:
We Were Here (prequel to Geoducks)
Geoducks Are for Lovers
Wanderlust
Happily Ever Now (TBA)

Wingmen:
Ready to Fall
Confessions of a Reformed Tom Cat
Anything but Love
Better Love
Small Town Scandal
The Last Wingman

Bewitched:
Bewitched
A magical short set in Salem, Massachusetts
Spellbound
A magical sequel to Bewitched
Enchanted
A magical continuation
Charmed
A magical conclusion

UP TO YOU

A LOVE WITH
ALTITUDE
NOVEL

DAISY PRESCOTT

Cover Design: ©SM Lumetta

Cover photos: ©Jacob Ammentorp Lund/Stocksy, ©Nyker, and ©twildlife

Editing: There for You Editing

Proofreading: Proofing Style

Interior Design & Formatting: Type A Formatting

For my husband

Because I was afraid of worms, Roxanne! Worms!
—Chris McConnell, *Roxanne*

ONE

MAE

"ARE THERE USUALLY penis straws at bridal showers? I thought those were banished to the drunken hours of shame and regret during the bachelorette party." Zoe's dark brows crease with worry. "I'm here for the cake. Obviously."

"Not even cake can fix this disaster. I can't be around my mother trying to suck on a tiny penis with a straight face." Not enough therapy in the world could help erase that memory.

Zoe's face falls at my dire vision for my cousin's bridal shower. "That can't happen. When we get there, we'll do some reconnaissance. If we find a bag of plastic dicks, we'll steal them. I'm pretty sure the Snowmass Mountain Club frowns upon a room full of women stirring their drinks with dicks. We'd probably all get banned."

She's right. Some things aren't done at the club. The whole place screams wealth, but using a restrained indoor voice. This isn't the typical pearls and cardigans uniform of the country club crowd. In the mountains we prefer everything to be more rugged and outdoorsy—both our men and our clubs. Mounted elk heads mix with diamonds and tennis in the summer; furs and skiing in the winter.

I park in the lot near the year round tennis courts. My vintage yellow VW Bug stands out in the crowd of Porsche SUVs, Teslas, and Land Rovers. We step out of the car and put on our game faces.

"Ready?" I roll back my shoulders and shake out my wrists. Bouncing in my wedge sandals, I throw a few punches along with some bobbing and weaving.

"Okay, Million Dollar Baby." Zoe ducks out of the way. "No need to cause physical harm. Let's assume the best. This could be a lovely afternoon filled with champagne and cake."

I stop pretending to be a boxer and give her a look. "You can't be serious. Have you met my family?"

"I am serious. Positive thinking. Visualize the best possible outcome." In her boho floral dress and booties, she's a lovely earth goddess with her dark hair in a messy braided bun.

"Which would be? I mean, other than turning around and leaving now." I twirl my keys around my finger, hoping she'll give in and agree with me.

Like her, I'm wearing a floral dress, but mine is mostly black with the occasional red rose. Zoe made me change out of the all black outfit I'd picked out, saying it was more suited for a funeral or a goth club. Either of those options sound like a better choice than sitting through a bridal shower with my pretentious extended family.

Undeterred by my grumpy attitude, Zoe continues, "I barely know the bride, so I have zero emotional investment in today. I'm hoping for several options of cake and more cake in the goodie bag."

"You're obsessed. You and Justin should get married. Then you can do a cake tasting. Or several."

Her dark lashes flutter as she thinks about this option. "I like your thinking, but a wedding is an expensive way to get cake when I can buy one any time I want. Lifetime commitment in exchange for buttercream is a little extreme, even for me."

I'm about to ask her if she and her cowboy have discussed marriage, when Sage's vintage, wood-sided Wrangler swings through the lot and parks a few spaces down the row. For someone who could afford any car in this lot, I love my friend even more for driving her old Jeep.

"Sorry I'm late." Sage jumps down from the driver's seat and then jogs over to us, her flowy, light blue maxi dress billowing behind her. Her face switches from apology to confusion, a line forming between her brows. "Why are you hanging around the parking lot? Are we sneaking edibles before we go inside?"

"Why? Do you have some?" I ask her, curious. "I could use a little help from a special gummy bear."

"No, I don't have edibles." She frowns at me.

"We should've planned ahead." I'm not upset at her. I've failed myself.

Sage nods in sympathy. "So if you're not tailgating by the cars, what are you doing out here?"

"Mae was warming up with some boxing moves before we go inside," Zoe answers.

Sage dips her chin and studies me.

"Stop with the look. My family isn't normal. Everyone will ask about my dating life and click their tongues about me still being single. Then give my mother pitiful looks of sympathy for having a spinster daughter. I'm older than dear cousin Twyla by four years. We're too young to imagine the horrors of having a spinster daughter. How will my mother ever recover from the shame?" I hold out my hands in a pleading gesture. "How?"

Sage gives me a side hug and Zoe joins us, closing the circle, both of them enveloping me with their arms.

"That's why we're here for you. None of us are married. We'll be sure to flaunt our naked left ring fingers whenever possible." Sage shows off her ringless hand. Zoe puts hers over it and bumps my hip to encourage me to add mine to the pile.

When I rest my palm on Zoe's hand, Sage says, "To the unmarrieds! Long may we live in sin!"

I laugh, but I really want to point out that while they're unmarried, they're not single. Like me.

"Let's do this." Sage links her arm with mine and then Zoe's. She may be petite, but her dancer's body is disturbingly strong.

River stone decorates the grand entrance, which sits under a huge portico held up with giant logs and thick beams. Obviously, size matters at the Mountain Club. The interior of the club is a mix of hunter green and tasteful plaid with more wood and flattering light cast from antler chandeliers and wall sconces. Somehow it manages to be both rustic and elegant.

The afternoon is warm enough that all of the French doors lining the far wall of the banquet room are open to the terrace facing the ski mountain and Mount Daly. Clear sunshine pools on the thick carpet and sparkles off of champagne flutes on the table.

Three tables are stacked high with pastel-wrapped gifts for the new couple. I drop off the small box with a gift card to La Belle Femme creperie near the top of the pile. Couples love crepes and it's one of the most romantic restaurants in Aspen. I might be biased since I work there.

Sage adds an envelope and winks at me. "Gift card from Cheeks. No way am I picking out lingerie for your cousin."

Equally tasteful women cluster together in small groups like flocks of colorful birds. Conversations and laughter are kept to a respectful murmur. An occasional burst of giggles elevates the general subdued feel. We linger near the door and I glance down the hall to the main bar, thinking if I'm in the building it should count as attending the bridal shower.

Subtly, I take a step back, shifting my weight to that foot to pivot in the direction of freedom.

"Uh huh. No escaping," Sage whispers. "Smile. We're all delighted to be here. Fake it if you have to."

Parting my lips, I show her my teeth.

"You look like you're thinking about eating me. Less menacing and more happy." She grins at me, leading me into the room.

Off balance, I tumble forward before catching my footing. When I glance up, my mother is shaking her head in disbelief and disproval.

Resigned, I tap Sage's arm. "I've been spotted. Suppose I should go say hello to my mom."

"We'll get you a drink." Zoe gives my hand a squeeze before releasing me.

Inhaling, I straighten my spine and pretend I have a stack of books on my head. Posture matters to these people. Slouching is considered a personal insult in my family. I believe my grandmother once told me that if you can't be bothered to keep your head up and your shoulders back, you must not have an ounce of respect for yourself or your parents.

I greet my mother with a kiss to her cheek and plaster on a reserved smile. "Hi, Mom."

"Mae. You look lovely." She touches my shoulder and covertly tucks my bra strap under the fabric of my dress.

"So do you. As always."

She brushes a hand over her perfectly tailored blue dress— simple, but obviously designer. Her hair has the same rich brown waves as mine, even if hers is colored to hide her grays. Once she joked she stole a lock of my hair to give to her stylist. I totally believe she'd do it.

"Mae and Margaret." A woman with a neat, blond bob air-kisses my mother in the general vicinity of her cheek. "I swear you two could be sisters."

"Oh, Gwendolyn. You're so good for my ego." Mom giggles.

I'm not sure Gwen is good for mine.

"Mae, you remember Gwendolyn Roberts. We've known her and her husband for longer than you've been alive. I believe you and her son were in school together."

For a moment I blink in silence at both women as they stare expectedly at me. *Roberts.*

"Landon Roberts?" I squawk, my voice a little too loud for polite company.

Sage appears next to me with a mimosa in each hand. "Ugh, that tool. Who is he screwing over now?"

The three of us still, like Sage is "It" in a game of Freeze Tag. I'm not sure my mother is breathing.

Unaware of the foot sticking out of her mouth, Sage scans the room. "I should warn the poor girl and give her a coupon for some self-esteem raising therapy."

My mother reaches for a strand of imaginary pearls at her neck. Not finding anything to clutch, she presses her hand over her heart.

I can't even look at Mrs. Roberts.

"Sage, this is Gwendolyn *Roberts.*" I emphasize the last name to clue her in.

Zoe chokes on her drink. I didn't see her join us. Coughing to clear her throat, she asks, "You're Landon's mother?"

Gwendolyn's attention bounces from my mother to me to Zoe, avoiding Sage all together. I can't look anyone in the eye, especially not my friends. The awkward tension is so off the charts I might burst out laughing.

Sipping my drink and scanning the room, I wait for someone to say something to dig us out of this social faux pas pit. After my earlier freakout, I'm both relieved and disappointed not to see anyone sipping their drinks with a pink phallus. We could use a dick distraction.

Sage pulls out her good breeding and extends her hand to Mrs. Roberts. "It's lovely to meet you. I'm Sage Blum, and

I apologize for my sense of humor. It's because I'm from Chicago."

Zoe's eyes widen with shock. "We're both from Chicago. What does that have to do with anything? It isn't like we were raised by the mob or feral cats on the shores of Lake Michigan."

My mother sighs with exaggerated disappointment. "Sage is one of the Chicago Blums. Of Bloom and Board."

Mrs. Roberts catches on to Mom's name-dropping, her scowl transforming into surprise as she takes Sage's hand. Nothing like millions in the bank to smooth over an awkward moment. "Oh, of course. I believe I met your parents at the Caribou Club several years ago."

"It's possible." Sage loosens her grip, but Mrs. Roberts holds tight like she finally has a lively one on her fishing rod.

"Didn't you date Landon?" my mother asks Sage, ignoring my not-so-subtle glare.

"Date is a strong word. We know each other. Aspen's a small town." She finally escapes Mrs. Roberts' hold.

"Sage's boyfriend is captain of the rugby team. They're living together. Cohabiting in the same condo. In sin." I don't want to leave any doubt they're more than roommates. I might as well announce they're having sex. "She's spoken for. Although Lee needs to put a ring on it, she's no single lady."

Four sets of eyes widen while words keep pouring out of my mouth.

"I think we get it, Margaret." My mother presses her hand on my forearm.

"Okay, didn't want there to be any confusion." I nod and try to sip from my empty flute. *Where'd my mimosa go?*

Zoe hands me her glass and I finish it.

"Are you dating anyone?" Mrs. Roberts asks me, sounding only vaguely interested.

"Uh, that would be a negative. It's the end of summer and

the dating pool has dried up more than the snowmelt. By late August, we're left with 'been there, done that' and the 'still not desperate enough to touch thats' of single people." I follow this up with a shudder.

"Mae," my mother hisses under her breath. To the mother of one of the untouchables, she says, "She's kidding."

"I wish," I say drily, taking another sip of mimosa.

"Then you're bringing a date for the wedding?" My mother's hand reaches for her imaginary pearls again. "You can't show up alone."

"I won't be alone. There are over three hundred invites to this shindig. I'll have my tribe with me, and I assume we'll all be sitting at the same table. No one will notice if I'm unchaperoned."

Mom and Mrs. Roberts exchange looks of horror. Mom lowers her voice to a whisper in case anyone is eavesdropping. "This isn't a night of debauchery at that tavern in Woody Creek, Margaret."

At the use of my proper name, I shoot Sage and Zoe a silent SOS.

"Isn't bringing a random guy to a wedding kind of weird? Watching two people pledge their undying love to each other is a lot of pressure on a date. I know weddings make people horny, but there are less awkward ways to get laid." I stare at my friends for confirmation.

With their eyebrows lifted, they manage to nod, but I'm not sure they agree.

Inside of my mother's brain, tiny blood vessels are exploding with every word that comes out of my mouth. Her face remains perfectly passive, but I can tell she's starting to simmer over this whole exchange. A small twitch appears beneath her left eyes.

"There's a simple solution to this issue," Mrs. Roberts speaks up.

Clearly, I misjudged her. She's on my side and is going to

tell my mother how silly the notion of a wedding date still is. After all, she's Landon's mother. She raised him. There's no way even she thinks he's dating or marriage material. Unless she's delusional, which is a possibility.

When she opens her mouth to continue, I hold my breath and prepare to mentally high five her. "Landon's single, too. He can be your date."

In my head, I hear the sound of tires screeching on asphalt as they try to avoid the impending impact. I imagine someone screaming and time slips into slow motion.

"No," I whisper at the same exact moment my mother gleefully says, "Oh, that's a wonderful idea."

"Then it's settled. I'll let Landon know when we have dinner tomorrow." Gwendolyn, my new least favorite person, smiles and takes a dainty swallow of her champagne. "How perfect," she says, delighted.

No, not perfect. The opposite of perfect. The word she's looking for is disaster or nightmare.

"I can't—" I try to decline, but my mother cuts me off.

"Wait. Mae can't wait. It's going to be the wedding of the year. Let's hope the aspen leaves don't drop early. Wouldn't it be perfect if they were at the height of their golden glory for the wedding? So divine."

The woman has clearly lost her mind. Never once in my twenty-seven years of life have I ever been excited about a wedding. It's like we've never met. How can she not know me at all?

"I—" Clearing my throat, I try again. "I'm not sure—"

This time Mrs. Roberts speaks over me. "Oh, wouldn't it be lovely if we get a light dusting of snow? All that gold and white everywhere? Do you know the wedding colors?" She directs her questions to my mother. "We should go find the bride and ask her."

"Oh, let's!" Mom's voice is giddy. Margaret London doesn't

do giddy. I'm now convinced this woman who appears to be my mother is actually a cyborg sent from the future to ruin my life.

Watching the two of them stroll across the room together like best friends, my stomach sinks and the bitter aftertaste of defeat coats my tongue.

"What just happened?" Zoe takes my glass and hands me another fresh mimosa. I don't know how she keeps them coming, but if she's bribed the waiter, I salute her.

Sage links her arm with mine and says in a low, somber voice, "I think Mae was set up on a date with Landon."

I'm too stunned to speak. My fingertips are cold. I might be going into shock.

Zoe's face falls at this possibility. "She doesn't have to go through with it, does she? We're adult women. No way are you obligated to be Landon's date because your moms decided this was a good idea. Your families don't believe in arranged marriage, do they?" All her questions jumble together.

"No, we don't have arranged marriages. I totally got played by my mother and Gwendolyn Roberts." I sigh and drink more mimosa.

"How is this even a thing?" Zoe asks. "You can't be forced to take that walking STD to your cousin's wedding."

"No one is going to make Mae do anything," Sage reassures me. "The wedding is six weeks away. You can find a real date between now and then."

"Easley would probably go with you." Zoe offers.

"He's the better alternative?" I ask, completely defeated. "Do they make suits large enough for gorillas? Why can't I be the sad spinster cousin who sits at the kids' table? I'll happily eat chicken nuggets and mac 'n' cheese."

My mother strolls over to our group with a satisfied feline smile on her face. Pressing her hand against my shoulder blade, she lowers her voice, careful to not be overheard. "Dear, it's one evening. The Roberts are a good family and it will make your grandparents happy to see you with a date. Sometimes we do things in life that don't thrill us but turn out to be worth the discomfort. Like thirty-four hours of labor to deliver a beautiful daughter."

She's serious if she dropped the labor and delivery guilt. Margaret London only pulls that story out when she means business. And she added in my grandparents, which is the cherry on top of this hot mess sundae.

"Fine, if he agrees, I'll do it. But I'm not going to beg him to be my date. I have some self-respect." I jut out my chin and meet her eyes.

"Wonderful," Mom exclaims happily, completely ignoring my reluctance. "Now that's settled, we can all enjoy this lovely party."

When she's gone, I turn to my friends. "Why do I think this was an ambush between Mrs. Roberts and my mother? I think they're in cahoots."

"Do we know if he's a momma's boy? Maybe Landon will refuse to obey his mother," Zoe asks, optimistically. "Sage?"

"How would I know?" Sage holds up her hands in defense.

"You slept with him. Did he call you Mommy or anything weird like that?" I feel bile rise in my throat.

Thankfully, Sage says, "Uh, no. He was more the kind of guy to ask for feedback every ten seconds on how awesome he was making me feel. It was exhausting and totally ruined my focus."

We all make the same frown.

"You don't have to sleep with him. Make sure you put that clause in the dating contract." Zoe laughs until she sees my face. "Too soon?"

"Didn't Mara go out with him when she first moved here?" Sage asks. "She survived."

"She was new and didn't know better. He ditched her

halfway through the meal after flirting with me. He's the worst. I should know since I grew up with the guy. I have decades of bad Landon stories," I add.

"At least you never slept with him." Zoe hands me a fresh cocktail.

I peer around her, looking for a tray of mimosas. Seriously, how is she doing this? Her purse is too small to hide even a half bottle of champagne let alone a carafe of juice.

"Thanks, bestie." Sage wrinkles her nose like she's smelled something horrible.

"You were going through a crazy phase. There was no discouraging you. And you ended up with the right guy. Maybe Mae will meet the man of her dreams by doing this? Stranger things have happened." Zoe gives me a sympathetic frown. "I fell in love with a rodeo cowboy. Never saw that coming."

Zoe and Justin are a new thing and at the height of the disgustingly happy phase of falling in love. Her ex was a horrible khaki-wearing tool and she deserves so much better. Thanks to me and my advice of getting back on the horse after her last relationship ended, she met Justin. I guess she took me literally, and not only rode the horse, but the cowboy, too. Can't blame her. Justin wearing a pair of chaps does cause spontaneous ovulation.

Unlike Landon Roberts who could cause a yeast infection with one touch.

If I'm going to be his date for this shindig, we're going to need to implement some ground rules.

Wedding date rule number one: no touching.

TWO

LANDON

AT LEAST I think there's a compliment somewhere in his statement.

"I'm fine. Thank you and fuck off." I flip him off with both hands, in case he misses my point. "I don't see you pulling tons of women. Or any."

The jerk shrugs. "I'm more of a quality over quantity guy. Always have been."

I scoff. "That's fancy bullshit for 'can't get laid' if I've ever heard it."

He dismisses my insult with a shake of his head. Water drips from the longer curls onto the leather. I don't know if he's showered recently or still wet from being on the river all day.

I don't let it go. "Right. Your problem is accessibility. I bet you live like a monk. Not a lot of women wandering around the back country."

"You'd be surprised. All that fresh air and sunshine is great for the libido." The smug bastard winks at me. His beard is scruffy, and with his shaggy, sun-bleached, overgrown hair, he looks like he lives alone in a mountain shack in Appalachia.

"After all of your time in the east, if you're into something kinky involving sheep or mountain goats, keep it to yourself." Yeah, I went there. He's been back for a couple of weeks and already he's annoying me. "Speaking of keeping to yourself, when are you going to find a place?"

He holds his hand over his heart. "You wound me, baby brother. Trying to get rid of me already? Afraid I'm cramping your style?"

"Aren't you too old to be sleeping on a pull out sofa?" I ask him.

"Man, this is my couch from Boulder. If anyone has a claim, it's me." He flops on the corner cushion. "I created this indentation. You've been sitting in the shadow of my ass."

"You want it back? Take it when you move." My hint is as subtle as one of my typical pick-up lines. "Thirty and no place of your own is pretty sad shit."

"No way. I'm afraid to know what's happened on this leather. It probably lights up like a fireworks display under blue light." Ignoring my jab about his current state of homelessness, he jumps up and strides into the kitchen. "You want a beer before we face our parents?"

Separated by a counter, the kitchen is basic and small, but none of us really cook, so it works. Easley and I lucked out finding a decent two-bedroom condo with two bathrooms we could afford without working multiple jobs. Skiing rules during the season and then rugby takes over our lives when the snow disappears. I don't have time to work a nine-to-five job like some suit in the city.

Like Aiden.

Or at least old Aiden before he flipped out. Guess the pressure of being successful got to him. He won't talk about it much, but do normal people quit their jobs, sell everything, and go hiking for five months? No, they don't.

Showed up here last week directly from Maine where he

finished hiking the Appalachian Trail. Something must be pretty fucked up in your life to make you want to walk over two thousand miles to try to get away from yourself.

I accept a beer from him. "You better shower before dinner. Mom will be mad enough you look like a mountain man. If you show up smelling like the river, her head might explode."

He pulls his shirt away from his chest and sniffs. "Okay, I might be a little past ripe."

"Easley after a match doesn't smell as bad as you do."

Sipping down his beer with one hand, he flips me off with the other. "I'm not showering for you. You two live like pigs with hoarding issues."

I scowl at him. "You're welcome to get your own place anytime, dear brother."

"You're going to have a paunch any day now." My jibe falls as flat as his stomach.

"Right. I'm not the one living off of a diet of beer and cheeseburgers like I'm still seventeen." He throws shade at my midsection.

"Mass is important in rugby. Size matters. That's probably why you've never played. Too skinny." I've put on another ten pounds over the season. We only have a few more matches before Rugby Fest in Aspen next month. I'll lose most of it before ski season, so he can give me all the shit he wants.

"I could still kick your ass, baby bro. You might be bigger, but I know your weaknesses." He turns up the steep, winding street to the house.

The modest two story house sits on slope across the road from the golf course. Not exactly the wrong side of the tracks, but not on the ski mountain. Like all real estate around here, it's still worth a fortune. Even down valley is getting outrageous.

Locals who didn't buy before the mid-eighties, aka before I was even born, are priced out unless we get lucky in the employee housing lottery.

After parking in the driveway, Aiden pauses before opening his door.

"Can we call a truce while we're here?" he asks.

"About what?" I ask, unsure which ongoing, lifelong argument he wants to put on hold for the evening.

"The jabs and the undercuts about me being homeless and living on your couch. It is temporary, I swear. Another couple of weeks tops. Just . . . cool it in front of Mom and Dad, please? It's bad enough they think I've lost my mind walking away from my job. It would be nice . . ." His voice lowers with resignation. "It would be nice to feel like I have at least one of you on my side."

"You're a bigger mess than I thought. I'm just giving you shit. Like we have our entire lives." Laughing, I lightly punch him in the shoulder. The grim expression on his face stops me. "Don't be so serious. You owe me a favor and someday you'll repay me. No big deal."

"I feel like I've made a deal with the Godfather. This isn't going to end well, is it?"

"I'd never put a horse head in your bed. Hide a trout in your lame dad rig, maybe." Off the top of my head, I can think of four places I'd hide a fish in here.

Laughing, he opens the door and gets out. "I should've moved back to my childhood room here."

I meet him by the hood. With a sympathetic clap on his shoulder, I lower my voice and tell him, "You can't. Mom turned it into her yoga studio."

"What did they do with yours?" He takes the steps to the front door two at a time.

"Kept it as a shrine to their favorite son. Duh." I pause

beside him before opening the door and stepping across the threshold, leaving him standing with his jaw hanging open. "All those sports trophies need a proper home."

"Asshole," he mutters as he passes me, digging his thumb into my back near my kidneys.

"Ouch. Fuck," I swear, a little too loudly apparently.

"Landon." Judgment and disappointment lace Mom's voice, but her face and tone brighten when she sees my brother behind me. "I'm so happy you're here, Aiden."

If we were eight and six, I'd stick my tongue out at my brother while Mom hugs him. I'm still tempted at twenty-eight.

"Hey, what about me?" I whine like a kid. "I'm the good son. The one who is on the undefeated rugby team, gainfully employed, and doesn't look like Tom Hanks in *Castaway* after he's lost his volleyball lover."

Aiden curses me out under his breath. Oops. I forgot about not mentioning his lack of employment. My bad.

Mom misses his foul language because she's staring at the mess on his head. "If you want, I can book you an appointment with the barber who trims your father's hair and beard."

"It's fine. I'm running rafts on the river, not making multi-million dollar real estate deals. No one cares if my beard is scraggly and my hair is unkept as long as I get them through the rapids safely. Some women like the hirsute look." He lifts an eyebrow at me in silent nod to our earlier conversation.

"I think your mom is saying you can be a guide and not look like Grizzly Adams." Dad appears in the doorway to his home office on the other side of the kitchen. Gray lightens his brown hair at the temple. He's wearing his typical uniform of a button-down shirt and jeans. He and Mom barely look over forty, but they're in their early fifties. Our mother is well preserved with potions and injections. Not sure what his secret is, but I hope the genes for it got passed down to me.

"Grizzly who?" Confused, Aiden and I ask at the same time. "Who?"

Our parents both groan, and Dad says, "Someone before your time."

"Maybe you can find him on Netflix or Hulu," Mom suggests.

Aiden shrugs at me. "Okay, sure."

Loudly sighing, Mom opens the fridge. "I'm having wine. Anyone else want something?"

"Been here three minutes and we're already driving her to drink. I think that's a new record," Aiden says, half-laughing as he joins Mom at the refrigerator.

"I blame your hermit hair and hideous face." I step around them both and grab a beer. In the crowded space, my elbow accidentally catches Aiden in the ribs.

His foot presses on top of my shoe when he steps away.

"When are the two of you going to outgrow these boyish antics?" Mom slides the cork from her favorite bottle of rosé. Gwendolyn Roberts is all about the 'rosé all day' movement. "I was a mother of two by the time I was Landon's age."

Aiden and I meet gazes. This is the beginning of her speech about us settling down and getting married in order to give her grandchildren. Apparently, there's only so much tennis a woman can play at the club.

"Speaking of weddings," she says as if we'd mentioned anything to do with marriage or nuptials at all this evening, "Twyla London is getting married in October. Didn't you go to school with her?"

Aiden sets his beer down on the marble counter. "Wasn't in my class."

How doesn't he remember her? "She was two years behind me. Tall. Curvy. Blonde. Went to CU. Competed at the Sochi Olympics for Biathlon, but didn't medal."

My brother stares at me with a blank expression.

"Cross-country skiing and shooting," I explain.

"I know what the Biathlon is, dufus." He picks up his beer and takes a long swallow. "What I'm curious about is how quickly you remembered all of those details from ten years ago."

Mom's eyes crinkle slightly in the corners. Impressive given how much Botox she pumps into her face. "I thought you knew her. I went to her bridal shower yesterday at the club."

"Who's the lucky guy?" Twyla and I aren't running in the same social groups. I don't think we've had a conversation in years, but that doesn't stop jealousy from flaring in my chest.

"Topher Tierney," Mom answers with a happy sigh. "Two of Aspen's power families joining together."

"Hold on. Topher and Twyla Tierney?" I bark out a laugh. "Lamest names ever. What kind of name is Topher?"

"I believe it's a shortened version of Christopher," Dad answers.

"Then why is he an asshole going by Topher instead of Chris?" I ask, completely serious. "He must've been bullied a lot in school."

"Landon." Mom isn't amused. "His great-grandfather is Albert Pfeiffer."

"Am I supposed to know him? I guess his life could be worse if his name were Topher Pfeiffer." Annoyed, I glance at Aiden for help. He shrugs, giving me nothing.

Dad frowns. "Pfeiffer and a few others, including Twyla's great-grandfather, developed the area as a ski destination after World War II. How do you not know this?"

"Why would I? Is this a history pop quiz?" I'm full on annoyed now and don't bother to hide it. "Who cares about ancient history?"

Mom sighs. "We live in a small community where social connections matter."

"Like I said, who cares? If they're so fancy, why is her cousin working at La Belle Femme? Mae's not living her life like local royalty." I chug my beer and then wipe off the overspill from my chin with the back of my hand.

"Honey, do I look like a wolf?" Mom asks Dad, reaching her maximum point of exasperation.

"No, still human." He busies himself with pulling steaks out of the fridge, along with a platter of shrimp laced on skewers for the grill.

"Sometimes I'm not convinced these boys weren't raised by wolves." Her gaze flicks from Aiden with his mountain hermit beard to me before settling on her wine glass. Deciding her glass is half empty, she adds more rosé and then follows Dad outside to the deck.

"Mae? Mae London?" Aiden asks, ignoring Mom's insults, or maybe he zoned out and missed them.

"What about her?"

"Nothing. I didn't know she was back in town." Rolling his head, he rubs his neck. "How is she?"

"Same, I guess. Hot. Holding a grudge against me. Working as a waitress. Still an amazing boarder when she's on the mountain."

"Huh," he says with a quick nod. "Cool."

"I guess." Finishing my beer, I head to the fridge for another. "You want one?"

He holds up his mostly full bottle. "Nah, I'm good. Should we join them out there?"

I nix that idea with a shake of my head. "Probably better to let her cool off for a couple of minutes first. I have no idea why she's all worked up about a wedding that doesn't involve her own children."

"I think you answered your own question. With both of us single, she has to find her joy somewhere else. You know she lives for big life events like weddings, holidays, and birthdays."

He's right. Gwendolyn loves big, emotional gatherings. "You left out funerals. She keeps a black suit dry-cleaned and ready should anyone keel over between here and Glenwood. The woman loves a good cry over a dead body."

"Speaking of dead bodies." Mom glowers from the open doorway. "Landon?"

I didn't even hear or see her come back inside. Stealthy.

"You're so dead," Aiden whispers into the mouth of his bottle.

"Yes, Mother dear?" I say, sweetness dripping off each word like honey. Fold my hands, I put on my wide-eyed innocent face.

"Save it for your revolving door of women." She places her empty glass on the island counter. "Do you have a date for the wedding?"

"What wedding?" I ask because I'm sure there is more than one upcoming wedding on her radar.

"The London-Tierney wedding, of course. Unless you've had one concussion too many and can't remember our conversation from five minutes ago." She isn't even a little amused by me right now.

"Why would I have a date for a wedding I'm not going to?" Crossing my arms, I lean against the counter. Mom's had too many glasses of rosé.

"You'll be invited. Invitations will be sent out this week."

"I think I'll be out of town. Playing rugby." There's no way I'm missing one of the last tournaments of the season for some society wedding.

"I thought the season ended in September with Rugby Fest?" Aiden's grin tells me he knows he just threw me under the bus.

"It does. Didn't Mom say September was the wedding? I'm sure I'm busy every weekend." I feel the solid ground of my excuse begin to slip out from under my feet.

"It's Columbus Day. That's mid October," she adds like I'm

an idiot, which apparently I am because I just blew my chance to get excused. "And you have to go because I've already told Mrs. London you'll be Mae's date."

"What?" I ask, my voice cracking.

"Why?" Aiden sets down his beer with too much force. The glass makes a loud cracking noise against the marble, but doesn't break.

"Yeah, why?" I echo him. "If I have to attend, I can bring my own choice of dates. I'm not some sad sack who needs his mother to set him up. Not like Aiden. Make Aiden shave off the recluse disguise and take her. If either of us needs help with the opposite sex, it's him, not me. I'm sure he doesn't have any other options."

I can't believe she thinks this crazy idea is going to fly with me. Anger heats my neck as I try to process why she thinks I'll go along with her plan.

"Fuck off, Landon," Aiden mumbles, wiping the bottom of his bottle with his open palm, checking for leaks.

Mom's lips curve with the start of a small frown. "Can you two be in the same place for more than five minutes without sounding like the dialogue from an R-Rated mob movie?"

"No," I say, sarcastically.

"It was a rhetorical question, dumbass." Aiden stares at the ceiling before mumbling, "I really need to get my own place as soon as possible."

"You could always move back in here. We have a guest suite on the lower level with its own bathroom." Mom touches his forearm, hope shining bright in her eyes.

"Thanks, but I can't move home with my parents. I'm thirty, and while I'm not even in the running for wedding date material, I do have some pride left." Aiden rests his hand over hers.

"Oh, sweetheart. I assumed you'd be gone before October. Plus, Landon and Mae are friends," Mom reassures him, her voice all lovey and doting.

"We are?" I ask. "Since when?"

"Aren't you? You grew up together and I know you run in similar circles in Aspen. When I ran into her at the bridal shower she was with Sage Blum, who dates your team's captain. You can go to the wedding as a foursome."

Yeah, she's definitely been pounding the pink wine if she believes any of that bullshit. I don't even know where to begin unraveling her words.

"First of all, Sage and I dated before she was with Lee. He's threatened to punch me more times than I can count, so ix-nay the idea of the four of us on a double date. Second, calling Mae and I 'friends' is kind of a stretch."

"Have you slept with her?" Mom asks, blunt and to the point.

Behind her Aiden's eyebrows lift with curiosity. Or amusement. He's obviously enjoying this too much.

"I don't kiss and tell." We haven't but it's none of my mom or brother's business.

"You can't bring some floozy you pick-up in a bar after a match to a wedding, Landon. Twyla and Topher have decided that if you haven't known your date for at least three months, no plus one. I've done you a favor." She gives me a closed mouth smile. "Otherwise, you'd have to go stag."

Flying solo surrounded by horny women all hopped up on love is one of the few reasons to go to a wedding. Open bar and free food are the other two.

"Did you and Mrs. London come up with this arrangement by yourselves? Does Mae agree?" I'm not saying yes to anything, but I'm curious if Mae was involved in this.

Given she's close friends with Sage and Mara, I doubt she's jumping at the chance to go out with me. Even if we did fool around in high school like the horny teenagers we were. Unfortunately we never closed the deal, but not for my lack of trying.

Current Mae's hot, way hotter than she was as a teenager.

Definitely more of a late bloomer than Twyla, and not as beautiful, but she isn't hideous. Far from it, actually. Long, dark hair with a killer smile, she's sassy enough to probably be wild in bed. My mom might be onto something with her meddling.

"She did agree." Mom won't meet my eyes. "Although her mother and I did come to the conclusion first."

"Soup's on." Dad enters the kitchen, carrying a tray of grilled steaks and shrimp. Seeing our grumpy faces, he pauses. "What did I miss?"

Aiden takes the food from him and places it on the table. "Mom's playing matchmaker for Landon because apparently he can't be trusted to find an acceptable wedding date who won't embarrass us all."

"No, I'm not." Mom carries the salad over to join the meat and then goes back for the dressings. "I'm trying to make life easier. And maybe avoid a public scandal at the most important event between now and the holidays. Aiden, will you take the baked potatoes out of the oven, please?"

Dad glances at Aiden before pulling out a chair and sitting. "Did your mother just compare Landon's dating life to the Kardashians? That can't be good."

"I'm impressed you know who they are." Aiden returns, carrying a plate with four baked potatoes, which he distributes on our plates before sitting next to Dad.

"I couldn't name them all, but I'm pretty sure our office brokered a house sale for one of them a couple of years ago." Dad sets a shrimp skewer on his plate.

Mom joins them, leaving me standing at the island with my mouth hanging open.

"Was that the one whose husband cheated on her?" She tosses the salad and serves herself before passing the bowl to Aiden.

They're like a freaking sitcom family right now.

Grumbling, I sit opposite Aiden. "That's it? You're all going to go on with your lives like Mom's behavior is normal? For the record, my life isn't a scandal. In fact, I love my life. Thank you very much."

"Steak or shrimp?" Dad asks.

"Salad?" Aiden holds the bowl for Dad.

"Landon, it's one night. Do it as a favor for your beloved mother. This wedding is the social event of the season and will be good for your father's business. Who knows? You might enjoy yourself more than you think." Mom stares me down.

Highly doubtful, but I give up fighting for the night. There's no point in arguing with my mother, not when she digs in her heels.

And maybe this is a good thing. Weddings make girls horny. If Mae is up for it, I'll be sure to show her the night of her life.

This might not be the worst idea ever.

THREE

MAE

LUCKILY, LA BELLE Femme is quiet tonight. Mid-week between summer and the height of fall foliage equals a lull in tourists. We have a steady flow of mostly locals, but by nine o'clock, all but two tables are empty.

Resisting a yawn, I drop off my final check with a smile. Once the last guests leave, I blow out the white candles scattered on the tables.

My tips for the evening aren't as terrible as I'd anticipated. This makes me happy as I walk down the quiet street to my apartment. It's owned by my uncle, who took pity on me when I moved back to town last year and gave me the family rate. At the time I thought I'd only be here for the ski season, but I've stayed.

Eventually he's going to realize my short-term rental is going on a year and probably kick me out. He can make more from a weekly rental during prime season than I pay in a three months.

Lost in thoughts of rent prices, my ringing phone startles me. I jump and let out a small scream, pressing a hand against my chest to calm my racing heart. With my other hand, I dig through my bag to find the phone.

An unfamiliar but local number is calling me. Normally, I'd send it to voicemail, but it might be someone at the restaurant, so I decide to answer it.

"Hello."

"Mae?" a man's voice asks.

"Who is this?" Uneasy, I glance behind me. No one is trailing me down the street. In fact, I can't see another person for blocks. *Safety in numbers*, I silently tell myself, and pull out my cat-shaped keychain.

"Is this Mae?" asks my anonymous phone friend.

"You go first since you made the call." Scowling at my phone's screen, I debate hanging up.

"It's definitely you." A familiar arrogant chuckle cracks the mystery of my caller.

"Landon." I keep my voice flat rather than growling like I want. I don't want to show emotion or give him any pleasure from causing a reaction in me.

"How'd you know it was me? Recognized my sexy voice?" he purrs, but instead of being sexy, it sounds like he needs to clear his throat of phlegm.

"Why are you calling me? Is someone dead?" Annoyance replaces my anxiety about a creepy, unknown caller. "Wait, how did you get my number?"

He chuckles again. "So many questions. No one is dead. I got your number from a mutual friend and I'm calling about our mothers."

I'm going to need to speak to my friends about privacy and boundaries. "You mean the wedding date? Our mothers are smoking meth if they think we're going to the wedding together." I laugh at the ridiculous idea, expecting him to chuckle again.

He doesn't. Completely serious, he says, "I think we should do it."

"It? Like have sex?" I screech. "Are you crazy?"

"I meant be each other's date for the big shindig. But if you're open to us fucking, what are you doing tomorrow night? Or if you have time tonight, I can be there in thirty minutes, but we'd have to be quick. Easley and I have plans to troll Little Annie's for tourists later." Now he's amused. At my expense.

"Keep it in your pants, Roberts. I'm not getting naked with you." Exasperated, I open the door to my building and climb the two flights of stairs to my apartment instead of taking the elevator.

"You're all breathy sounding. Are you touching yourself thinking about it?" Chuckling at his own joke, he's so full of himself.

Acidic bile tickles the back of my mouth.

"You're unbelievable. I'm climbing stairs. Is there a point to this call other than to harass me?" Once inside of my apartment, I toss my keys in the bowl on the console table and drape my bag on one of the hooks on the wall.

"You're no fun. Okay, I'm serious about getting together tomorrow or later this week to hang out and discuss our up-coming date."

I stare at myself in the mirror above the narrow console table and mouth, "He's serious."

Switching over to speaker, I set my phone next to the bowl so I can remove my jacket and shoes. "No need. I'm giving you the out. I'm planning to have the stomach flu that week-end. Food poisoning from a bad oyster. Migraine. Whooping cough. Shingles. The avian flu. Whatever seems most plausible at the time. I'll improvise. Apologies in advance for canceling on you last minute. Feel free to use this to garner sympathy from a lonely bridesmaid. Or two. You do you. Bye, Landon." My finger hovers over the screen about to disconnect the call.

He's laughing again. "I forgot how hysterical you can be, Mae."

I'm not trying to be funny. This conversation is a disaster.

"All joking and brilliant sexual innuendoes aside, are you free tomorrow?" he asks.

"Why?" In my socked feet, I pad over to the kitchen with my phone in my hand.

"Let's hang out. It's been too long."

"I thought we covered this already. You're free. I release you from being my date." Sighing, I decide to have a glass of wine.

"Come on, I'll be a perfect gentleman. We'll have fun." I don't ask if he's talking about tomorrow or the wedding.

"I'm working tomorrow." It's the truth, not an excuse.

"We can meet up after. One drink. I'll pay."

His relentless refusal to let this go surprises me. Curiosity piqued, I dismiss my gut, and say, "Okay."

I'm saying yes, but not for a free drink. No, I'm not that desperate. However, I am a sucker for a good redemption story. Back in high school, we hung out a lot. Sometimes he was the same jerky asshole he is now, but there were times when it was only us that he was nice, funny, and interesting. Maybe somewhere beneath the overdeveloped muscles and arrogance, that guy still exists.

Stranger things have happened.

"Okay? You're saying yes?" Shocked, he loses his cocky attitude for a second.

"To the drink only. I should be done with work around nine. I'm not saying yes to the wedding date. Deal?" I take the bottle of wine and a glass with me over to the small love seat.

"Deal. I'll pick you up."

"This isn't a date, Landon. Tell me where to meet you."

"The Red Onion okay?"

"Great. See you then. Night." I don't wait for him to say anything more and disconnect the call.

"I'm voluntarily hanging out with Landon Roberts." I lift my glass in a toast. "To the end of times."

FOUR

MAE

I LOVE MY hometown at night. Fairy lights illuminate the double row of aspen and pine trees down the center of the pedestrian only section of Hyman Avenue. Twin streams flanked by grass complete the woodland feel in the middle of downtown. The soft glow from shop windows creates a magical feeling that has nothing to do with wealth or social status no matter the cost of the goods displayed inside.

A dress catches my eye and I pause to study it more closely. It would be perfect for the wedding, and it isn't even black. The silk fabric is a deep, emerald green. Without lace, or anything sparkly, the long dress is an elegant column. Classy, but not boring. I'm in love with it. And then I notice the gold lettering on the glass.

Prada.

"Why does everything I love have to be unattainable?" I press my palm against the window in a sad farewell. I'll check out Aspen's finest thrift store and say a prayer I can find something half decent in the designer section. Women donate the most outrageous clothes and shoes in this town. Lucky for me and my wallet.

A few people loiter outside of the Red Onion, smoking cigarettes, and from the skunky smell in the air, pot. One guy in a popped collar waves around a fancy vape pen. Of course he does. He's probably a friend of Landon's. Who rocks a popped polo shirt collar these days? Apparently, that guy right there. He's bringing back the preppy asshole look even though no one has asked him to.

I quickly pass the dude bros to walk inside. The regular bouncer, Conner, sits at the bar, chatting up a female bartender I don't recognize. She's blonde and tall, with a healthy tan like she spends as much time outdoors as possible.

"Shouldn't you be guarding the door?" I slide onto a bar stool a few down from the bouncer. There's maybe ten people scattered around room.

"Hey, Mae. I think I can handle the crowd tonight while sitting down." Conner flashes a smile, revealing a gap between his front teeth. "What brings you to the Onion tonight? Hot date?"

"Meeting Landon." No point in telling him anything different. He'll find out soon enough who's the other half of this school night rendezvous.

The hand holding his beer freezes inches from his mouth. "You and Landon are dating?"

"Never said it was a date." I catch the bartender's eye and order a Fat Tire.

"Didn't you two have a thing in high school?" Conner must be bored because he won't let it go.

"Ancient history. Landon and I are a shining example of a healthy relationship between exes. It's all about boundaries." Which are maintained by never hanging out together.

"You went out with Landon Roberts, too?" Placing my pint on a napkin in front of me, the bartender gives me a sympathetic smile.

We need a secret sign or pin for the Sisterhood of the Unfortunate.

"My deepest sympathies," I tell her with a soft smile.

"First beer's on me. Want me to start a tab for you?"

"Nah. I'm not going to hang out for long. Thanks for the drink. I'm Mae."

"Anika. Nice to meet you."

I lift the glass in her honor. "To better men. May we find them and date them."

She clinks her water bottle against my beer. "Amen."

Landon shows up on time, which is another unexpected twist to this strange adventure. He doesn't seem like the punctual type—too narcissistic to care about little things like respecting other people's time.

He greets Conner with a hand-clasp and a back slap.

If they grunted and thumped their chests, it wouldn't surprise me. Conner isn't nearly as thick as Landon, but they're probably the same height.

Taking the stool next to mine, Landon gives me an awkward half-hug. Like we're friends, buddies, pals.

I don't hug him back.

The contact lasts longer than a few seconds and I begin to worry he's incapable of picking up on body language and subtle clues.

Finally releasing me, he focuses on the bartender. "Hey, Anita. How's it going?"

My eyebrows lift as I wait for her to correct him. She doesn't, but her lips flatten together in a thin line of annoyance.

"IPA?" she asks, ignoring his question.

He nods, sweeping a hand through his short, blond hair like he's starring in a beer commercial.

Once she pours his beer and places it on the bar, Anika strolls down to the far end by Conner, putting as much distance between herself and Landon as possible.

He's oblivious because I swear he's trying to look down my cleavage.

"Eyes a little higher, Roberts."

He meets my stare and doesn't appear the least bit sheepish. "Haven't seen you at any rugby matches. You boycotting the club or something because Lee ditched the team mid-season to take his girlfriend on vacation?"

I notice he doesn't use Sage's name, yet from his bitter tone, he blames her for Lee not playing a few matches this summer.

"Scheduling conflicts. Trust me, I've been devastated to miss the opportunity to watch men thrash on each other over a ball," I say drily.

Landon misses, or ignores, my sarcasm, and launches into a monologue about the club's recent wins.

There are dozens of things I'd rather be doing right now than listen to Landon retell every excruciating detail of his last three rugby matches. Despite taking tiny sips of my beer every time he says scrum, only a third of it is left. I'm sure somewhere, someone uses scrum as slang for scrotum. If not, it's a lost opportunity.

These are my top five preferred activities over hearing a rugby play-by-play:

Getting a cavity filled without Novocaine.

Using an epilator to remove my pubic hair.

Tweezing Easley's back.

Shopping with my mother.

Eating sea urchin.

Out of all of these, I'd put shopping with my mother last.

"Sorry. That was probably way more than you wanted to hear," Landon apologizes. "Thanks for meeting me tonight."

"Sure. It's on my way home." *Ah, home.* I wave away his thank you.

I stretch, prepared to fake a yawn so I can claim exhaustion and put an end to the night.

His eyes widen slightly. "I forgot you lived in town. Must be nice."

"My uncle owns the building. There's no way I could afford to live by myself waiting tables and volunteering." We're not all trust fund kids around here even if we come from supposedly wealthy families.

"Again, must be nice," he says, flatly, and then sips his beer.

"Cut it out. We grew up together. You know my family, I know yours. Isn't that why we're here tonight? Because our families are friends and both conspiring against us?"

"What? I was just saying it's nice that you have a place in town." His tone switches from over-the-top flirty to his typical teasing. "Makes it easy for quick hook ups."

I don't mean to snort, but I do. "You're a beast. Is sex all you ever think about, Landon?"

"Pfft. No." He sits up straighter.

"Tell me two other subjects that float through your head on a regular basis."

Stalling, he drinks more of his beer. "Rugby and money. I'll throw in snowboarding as a bonus."

At least we have one thing in common besides our shared childhood. There's not a lot to say about snowboarding when there's no snow on the ground. Ignoring his smug smirk, I reply with snark, "Congratulations for being well-rounded and deep."

"You're welcome. I am capable of having a conversation, Mae. Contrary to what most people believe, I'm not a complete asshole. Even if my brother would say otherwise."

Finally a topic I'm interested in. "How is Aiden?"

"Living on my couch like a freeloader." He scoffs. "Washed up at thirty. Imagine that."

"What?" I'm sure I've misheard him.

Aiden moved away after he graduated and rarely comes home except for the holidays. Or so I've heard. Not like I've been stalking him and his life for years via random online posts, local gossip, and chance sightings. As far as I can tell he doesn't have his own accounts on social media, which makes tracking him more difficult and frustrating.

I'm not harboring a secret love for the older Roberts brother. It's more fascination than obsession. Four years older than me, he's always seemed more adult and worldly. Couch surfing doesn't fit with the image of him I've created in my head over the years.

"He's back? Since when?" I ask, attempting to keep my voice normal.

"For now. Called me a couple of weeks ago from Maine asking if he could stay with me." He shrugs.

"Maine?" Clearly, my detective skills suck. "Doesn't he live in San Francisco?"

My brain to mouth filter sucks, too.

Landon squints at me like he's trying to sniff out the truth. "He did. Before he cracked and had his mid-life crisis early."

"What does that mean? Like a mental breakdown?" I fail to keep the interest from my voice.

"Something like that. Had to take some time away from the world to find himself. All I know is now he's working as a river guide and sleeping in our living room. Does that sound like the behavior of a genius tech CEO? The golden boy isn't looking too shiny these days." Bitterness coats every word he speaks.

Growing up, Landon lived in his brother's shadow. In a way, we all did. Big personalities run in the Roberts family, but Aiden was special. Valedictorian in high school, top of his class at Colorado University, angel funded start up at twenty-three, and beyond the resume, handsome, smart, funny, and kind. So handsome and fit. Maybe because he's older, but he always seemed more grown up, more together than any guys in my class or Landon's. Aiden Roberts was the complete package, worthy of every teenage girl fantasy had about him.

Disappointment and sadness curl up together on my chest.

Like seeing a favorite celebrity being an asshole in person or transforming from heart throb to hot mess, my old crush dissipates and fades with this new reality.

"Nice of you to take him in when he's having a hard time."

"He's my brother. I'm not going to let him be homeless." Landon sounds resigned.

Wow, I had no idea Aiden had fallen so far. I want to ask if he has a drug problem. Or a gambling addiction. Or spent all his money on high priced escorts from former Soviet countries. I cross off that possibility immediately. Why would a good looking, successful guy like Aiden have to pay for sex? Unless he's into really weird, kinky stuff. I debate which would be worse: escorts for kinky sex or spending all of his money on obscure rap albums. Even I've played around with fluffy hand-cuffs and being tied up. After the Fifty Shades phenomenon, who hasn't? Besides my mother because I can't live in a world with that knowledge.

"Is he going to stick around for a while?" I actually feel sympathy for Landon. *What's happening to me?*

"Who can say? Rafting season's going to end soon. Easley's starting to get cranky about the apartment being too crowded. I'm giving Aiden through the beginning of October to figure out his shit." Landon finishes his beer. "Enough about my sad sack of a brother. How do I convince you being my wedding date is the best decision you can make?"

"In my life? This week? This year? What time parameters are you putting on this ranking?" I don't know how many times and ways I can let him know I think this is a terrible idea.

"You are really funny. I like that about you. Come on. Going together will make our mothers happy. Don't you want to bring a little joy into your mom's life? If the mom guilt doesn't work on you, think about the FOMO you're going to have. Everyone we know will be going. Think of all the free food and top shelf liquor. You know this is going to have an open bar."

In spite of thinking he's generally an ass, I smile at his genuine compliment. I'm beginning to think maybe he isn't the worst. After all, he did take in his sex addicted, broke brother, and he wants to make his mom happy.

I begin to seriously consider his offer. "Getting my mother off of my back about finding a husband would be a gift," I say, softly and mostly to myself. "I'm not sure how many more sighs and frowns of disappointment I can handle in one day. If she didn't already have Botox, I'd buy her a round of injections for her birthday. I'm sure she blames me for all of her wrinkles and gray hairs."

Tipping his head back, he laughs loud enough Conner and Anika shift to stare at us. "You're hysterical. You know why funny women are the best?"

Before I can answer, he says, "They're usually great in bed."

And he ruins it again.

"Jeez, Landon. It always comes back to sex with you."

"Then give in and have sex with me," he whispers, leaning closer. "If we fuck, we'll relieve some of this built-up sexual tension. We can go to your apartment right now. Then you won't maul me at the wedding."

His breath smells of beer and future regret.

I press my hand against his shoulder to not so gently remove him from my personal space. "Not happening. You're really terrible at flirting, you know."

Honestly, he's so awful, I'm not sure if he's even trying to flirt.

"Says who? I do all right with women. Right, Anita?"

Anika shakes her head. "It's Anika, and she's right."

"Then why did you go out with me?" Deep lines crease his forehead.

She twists her mouth before speaking. "I wouldn't say we

went out. You were a hot rugby player. I was horny. Perfect combination. There wasn't a whole lot of talking that night, so I didn't realize my mistake until later."

Landon's face falls. "Mistake?"

Anika's eyes meet mine and she grimaces. "That might sound too harsh, but we've slept together and you just called me by the wrong name."

How Sage put up with him for more than a date or two blows my mind. The only answer that makes sense is he's getting worse with age, instead of better. Instead of being a fine wine or cheese, he's a stale, three-day-old loaf of bread or a questionable almond that leaves a bitter aftertaste.

There must be some tiny seed of decency buried deep inside of him, under all the composted bullshit and ego.

He swallows the last of the beer and then frowns.

Damn it, now I'm feeling sorry for him. Don't, I tell myself. Don't open your mouth. Keep your feelings to yourself. Landon Roberts isn't your responsibility. You can't change someone who doesn't want to change themselves. You do not need a pet project.

Do I listen to myself? Nope.

"I'll be your date for this over the top display of wealth and pretension on one condition." I touch the back of his hand.

"Does it involve having sex?" Flashing his teeth, he gives me a wolfish grin.

"Not a snowflake's chance on a hot summer day. Sex is off the table." I hold my hand in front of his face. "Don't say whatever you're thinking."

His deep exhale of breath brushes over my palm. "Fine."

"Between now and the rehearsal dinner, you need to prove you can be a decent human. I'd say gentleman, but I don't want to set the bar too high and have you fail. This isn't punishment for prior douchebaggery. I'm doing you a favor. Hell, I'm taking one for all of womankind. You think you can rein in your dickhead tendencies?" Goading him with an insult, I smile at him, hoping he'll tell me to fuck off and find another date.

"You should listen to her," Conner pipes up from his corner. "Man, your reputation is shit. You're lucky there's a constant flow of new arrivals in this town or you'd probably never get laid again."

Bouncer-man's throwing down some harsh truths. Grinning, I give him a thumbs-up.

"Deal?" I hold out my hand to shake on it.

"What do I have to do?" He slides his index finger back and forth over my palm while staring into my eyes.

"To start, stop doing shit like that. You don't always have to be making a move. Relax and be yourself, the real Landon." Whoever that is.

"And what's in it for me?" He purses his lips into a pout.

"Happiness? Love? A life filled with quality over quantity?"

"Whoa. Slow down, Mae. I never said anything about falling in love with you. It's one date. And some casual sex."

I swear I'm going to slap him, and I don't believe in violence. This is pointless. Beyond frustrated I've wasted time on a lost cause when I could've been sleeping, I stand up and reach for my wallet to tip Anika. "You're on your own, Roberts."

His laughter stops my movement. "I was kidding. I can play nice. Promise."

Exasperated, I stare up at the ceiling, knowing I'm going to regret helping him. Somehow this will backfire in my face.

Conner speaks softly to Anika, but not quiet enough that I can't overhear him bet her a twenty Landon crashes and burns.

While I'm counting tin ceiling tiles, a warm hand wraps around my elbow. "I'll be the perfect gentleman. Swear on the championship cup. You'll be so impressed, I'm going to blow your panties off."

Squeezing and releasing my balled up fists, I slowly exhale

a breath and focus on his face. Devilish comes to mind when I see his expression, his eyes glimmering with mischief. "Ground rules. No mention of sex. Or panties. Or nudity. No flirting with, or trying to pick up, other women in front of my family and your parents at the rehearsal dinner or at the wedding."

"You'll have my full attention." He picks up my hand and cradles it in his before placing a soft breath of a kiss on my knuckles.

"Dial it back to a seven, Romeo."

"We should hang out again before the wedding. Practice my human decency and all that. I'll call you."

"You're probably right, but keep in mind we're not dating."

A single eyebrow lifts in challenge. "I have a feeling I'll be able to change your mind."

Laughing, I put on my jacket and back away from him. "Yeah, good luck with that."

There's no way I'm going to fall for Landon. Not even if he somehow turns from wart-covered frog into a real prince.

Like a viral cat video on social media, I replay this disaster of an evening over and over in my head as I walk home. The dark shadows of the mountains loom ominously in front of me. I think I've just made a deal with the arrogant, womanizing, evil, blond devil with the mischievous glint in his eyes.

FIVE

MAE

I PRESS THE pads of my fingers against my temples. "My curiosity got the better of me. I thought I saw a glimpse of humanity somewhere in the depths of his soul. Maybe he's deeply insecure and needs to build up a sense of self-worth."

Sage practically does a spit take on her wine. "Or a narcissist with an overinflated ego."

"He does remind me of Narcissus. Can't you see Landon staring at himself in a reflective pool?" Zoe asks.

"Or a mirror," Sage adds with an eye roll.

"Or a window if the glass is reflective enough." Mara almost gets the words out before she cracks herself up.

We're sitting on the deck of Sage's condo, enjoying a warm Labor Day evening before the cold weather returns. The calendar barely says September, but the nights are becoming chilly. A crackling fire in their outdoor fireplace warms the small space, adding to the feeling fall is right around the corner.

"His ability to appear human is how he lures you in. He's like one of those fish with the dangly bit hanging off of his head that tricks innocent, littler fishes, drawing them closer until it can open its jaws of death and eat them." Mara's eyes are wide like she's telling a ghost story.

"You've been watching *Blue Planet* again, haven't you?" I ask her. As a veterinarian, the woman is obsessed with all things animals. Except horses, but that's a long story.

"*Blue Planet 2*, thank you very much. We can learn a lot from animals and their mating rituals, not to mention predators on both land and in the sea." Mara threads a marshmallow onto a skewer. She brought the entire s'mores set up tonight. "Landon's more of a shark type. You can't fight genetics and deep-rooted instincts by force. You have to slowly reprogram him. Like training a dog. Reward the good behavior and try to ignore the bad behaviors like barking for attention."

"Landon definitely does that. He'll also hump any dog in the neighborhood if given the chance." Sage stares into the fire, shaking her head. "I can't believe I went out with him for longer than a minute."

"He *is* extremely good looking. Like a missing link between Chris and Liam," Mara says in support of Sage's lack of asshole radar. "Does he have a twin? He could be the evil one and somewhere out there is a good version. Maybe with amnesia after they were separated at birth."

"This isn't a soap opera," Zoe joins the conversation from her chair closest to the fire.

"Are you sure?" I ask, handing my skewer to Mara for a marshmallow. "I'm almost certain we're living in a real life version."

"Doesn't Landon have a brother?" Sage inquires nonchalantly, sipping her glass of wine.

"Yes. Older by two years. And from the sound of it, he's a hot mess." I fill them in on what Landon told me about his brother.

"Holy cats," Mara swears. "Landon's the good one? Yikes."

"Appears that way. Too bad, because growing up, Aiden was the better looking brother. Nicer and super smart." I frown, still feeling sad that he turned out to be a mess.

"If I've learned anything from watching ocean documentaries, there are plenty of fish in the sea. Not as many as there once were, but enough to still provide lots of viable options." Mara passes my skewer back to me, loaded up with three marshmallows. "Survival of the fittest and all that natural order jazz."

"Thanks for the pep talk, Dr. Doolittle." I adore my friends, but they're nuts. None of us are normal or boring and I wouldn't change a thing about any of them. "I know you're all coupled off and probably busy with coupling activities, but the fundraiser party for the Aspen Coalition is next Sunday afternoon. I've added you all to the guest list. Free drinks and snacks from three to five."

"Justin and I are going. His grandmother is on the board." Zoe wraps her long cardigan tighter around herself.

"Lee and I will be there, too," Sage confirms.

"Jesse's working on a job down valley, but I can be your date," Mara offers.

"Deal." I'm happy to go with Mara.

"Maybe you should invite your social experiment," Sage suggests. "I'd love to see if your advice has had any affect yet."

"Doubtful. It's been only been three days." I remind myself to research the symptoms of Whooping Cough in case I need to fake an illness for the wedding weekend.

※

Waitressing and volunteering isn't where I thought I'd be at twenty-seven. It's a trade-off for living in Aspen. In L.A., I worked all the time, barely had enough energy leftover on the weekends to run errands and adult. Life became a never ending treadmill. The faster I ran, the further behind I felt. I swear my old boss fed off of the stress and tears of her staff.

After ending up in the ER with a panic attack, I had enough

and quit my job at a boutique communications agency. Then I made the most difficult call of my life to tell my parents I wanted to move home to spend the winter snowboarding.

That went as terrible as I imagined, but I came back anyway. I'm still not sure if I'm going to stay, but while I'm here, I want to make a difference even if it's a tiny droplet of water falling in a constantly rushing river.

Today's fundraiser is a kick-off event for our fourth quarter push for donations, which culminates with a fancy gala at the Hotel Jerome in December with celebrity ambassadors and national press coverage. Hosted on the rooftop of the new museum building downtown, this afternoon should be much more low key with mini burgers and local craft beers and spirits on the simple menu.

A four piece bluegrass band sets up on the side opposite the view of Ajax Mountain. The exposed roof trusses create wavy shadows over both the indoor and outdoor spaces separated by tall glass walls that have been opened on this warm late summer day. Given the casual nature of the party, only a few tall bar tables are scattered around, encouraging people to mingle and move around.

My job tonight is to take pictures and post them on our social media. I might even do a couple of short live videos as well as a short interview with Wilhouby Parker, our director. Anything to create buzz about the Coalition and the event.

Guests begin arriving shortly before three. On cue, our catering staff appears with trays of drinks and finger foods. I recognize Anika from the other night and wave.

She smiles back and weaves her way over to me. "I didn't know you worked the catering circuit, too."

"I don't. I'm here as part of the Coalition staff."

"Oh, sorry. I saw your black dress and assumed you were one of us. In that case, do you want a mountain julep? Locally distilled bourbon, ginger spiked simple syrup, and a sprig of alpine mint." She swings her tray in front of me.

"Is alpine mint a real thing?" I take a copper mug and bite into the candied ginger garnish.

"No, but don't tell the fancy people." With a jerk of her head she indicates the growing crowd. "They like to feel like they're having something special that only money and being in Aspen can buy."

"So true." We share a laugh.

Her smile falters as she stares over my shoulder. "Of course he showed up."

I twist my neck and spot Landon's blond head above the crowd. With his height and broad shoulders, he's hard to miss.

"Who's the rugged mountain man who walked in with him?" Anika whispers excitedly, pointing at the guy standing next to Landon.

"I don't recognize him. New rugby player? He's tall enough to be part of the club." Almost the same height as Landon, he has thick, shaggy hair bleached lighter blond on the ends by the sun. With his back to me, I can't see more than his hair and shoulders.

"He kind of looks familiar," she continues to whisper from behind her cupped hand. "Maybe if he turns around we'll recognize his face. Let's move closer and find out."

Before I realize what she's doing, she takes my hand, leading me through the sparse crowd.

Not wanting to be spotted by Landon yet, I drag my feet to slow her down. "This is close enough."

I now have a good profile view of the mystery man. Long, strong nose. High cheekbones. Tan skin that's lighter around his eyes from wearing sunglasses, not tanning booth goggles I hope. And a full, bushy beard that looks to be as unkempt as his hair.

"Wow, he's a mountain I'd like to climb and plant my flag on his peak," Anika purrs beside me.

"Down, girl. If he's with Landon, he's probably bad news like his friend." She's right—there's something familiar about his face.

I'm outright staring at him when he turns his head to face me full on. Our eyes lock for a second before I quickly look away.

"Definitely stay away from him," I whisper, walking in the opposite direction. My heart slams against my ribs and my breath comes out choppy.

"Why?" Anika catches up with me. "He could be gorgeous under the man fur. Nothing a pair of sharp scissors, a razor, and some shaving cream can't fix."

"If you think Landon is a bad egg, meet the older Roberts brother, Aiden. He makes our mutual friend seem like a saint."

This revelation apparently piques her interest. Instead of running for the hills, she stops following me and straightens her shoulders.

"I love a good bad boy." A knowing smile twists her mouth. "I think I'll work that side of the room. See if anyone needs anything."

Apparently, Anika has a type. Tall, blond, and a terrible idea. Like a moth to a flame that will most certainly burn her, she can't resist the pull. There's no point in me telling her Aiden is broke and probably a gambling addict with weird sexual predilections. Nothing I can say will deter her if she already has a thing for bad boys and didn't learn her lesson after Landon.

My eyes track her through the crowd until she stops in front of the Roberts brothers. Landon glances up and smiles when he sees me. I give him a small wave and then turn in the opposite direction.

This is a work function for me and I need to make sure I'm not neglecting my official duties, whatever those might be.

Inviting Landon wasn't my smartest idea. I had no idea he'd bring Aiden to the event.

Best to avoid them if at all possible tonight.

I scan the crowd for my friends, hoping they're here and can create a buffer. One good growl or scowl from Lee should ward off any unwanted attention. I don't find my girls, but my eyes are drawn back to the group where I spotted Landon.

Once again, I find myself the focus of Aiden's stare. The intensity surprises me and I glance behind myself to double-check he isn't focused on the mountain view or another person at the party. When I return my attention to him, he smiles. At least I think he does, because with the thick beard, it's hard to tell for sure.

SIX

AIDEN

I FEEL LIKE this happens in almost every Bond or Bourne movie I've ever watched. Never thought it was a real thing. Not until tonight. Not until I locked eyes with the beautiful brunette with the warm eyes and killer smile.

Landon dragged me to this event with the excuse he needs my help. He didn't give details other than my role for the evening will be to keep him from making an ass out of himself. I'm not sure I'm up for the challenge. Not even James Bond has the arsenal of weaponry needed to stop my brother from himself.

We've been at the museum for ten minutes and I have to assume he's fine because I haven't spoken to him since we arrived. Occasionally, I get a glimpse of the top or back of his head across the room, or his familiar laughter rises above the din of superficial conversations. There hasn't been any screaming, fighting, crying, or other outburst of emotions inappropriate to a fancy Aspen shindig, so all must be well.

I wander through the party, nodding hello to the few people who recognize me while eating tiny, but tasty foods, and sampling small glasses of craft beers.

The rooftop garden is stunning. The architects optimized

the height of the building to fabricate the illusion we're above it all, and at the right angle, downtown disappears from view completely. There's only us and the dramatic backdrop of Ajax. I stroll over to the edge and a stare at the grassy ski slope. Away from the crowd and din of voices, I can breathe easier.

After spending five months essentially alone in nature, I easily become overwhelmed by humanity these days. For months, having a conversation with more than a handful of people over the span of a week was rare. Even the times the trail crossed through a town, I rarely sought out social contact. When I flew home from Maine, the small Portland airport was too crowded with the tired, huddled masses. I can't fathom living in the city. My neck itches at the thought of wearing a tie again.

Thankfully, Aspen is a casual town despite its reputation for being ritzy. I can get away with jeans and a fresh white shirt instead of wearing a suit.

I chuckle to myself. If young, ambitious Aiden could see me now, he'd probably head to the bar, order a double shot of bourbon, and tell the bartender to leave the bottle.

When I left this valley twelve years ago, I swore I'd never move back full time. Sure, I dreamed of buying my own multi-million dollar house here . . . one I'd only use a few weeks of the year for skiing. Because I could. At eighteen, I had a fire under my ass and dollar signs in my eyes.

The rest of the world might know this area for its celebrity visitors and billionaire residents, but it's still a tiny, mountain town. Too small for my ego and my brother's to co-exist peacefully.

Now the prodigal son has returned. When I woke up a year ago and decided to turn my life upside down, shake the shit out of it, and walk away from everything I built in Silicon Valley, I didn't plan to come back here and have the same job I had during summer breaks in college.

It was never one of my goals in life to be sleeping on my brother's couch.

Or become his personal life guru.

More like a romance coach for the clueless.

Is that a thing? Can I design an app for that? It's tempting. Landon isn't the only guy I know over twenty-five who still hasn't figured out how to talk to girls like they're human beings and not just sexual conquests.

After we left our parents' house on Sunday, Landon seemed resolved to make the best of our mother's meddling. Confident he could use her set-up to his advantage, he informed me he asked Mae out for a casual drink to test the level of her interest. Before he left to meet her, he cockily told me not to wait up for him as he'd probably not be coming home until morning.

Gotta give him some props for confidence, even if he has nothing to back it up. He was home by eleven-thirty and that's with the half hour drive from Aspen back to the apartment.

His bad mood obvious, he woke me up stomping around the kitchen, opening and closing doors, getting ice out of the freezer, filling his glass from the faucet, and then dropping the entire damn thing on the floor.

He wasn't amused by my amusement at his early return home. After giving him shit for a few minutes, I got more details out of him about the evening.

If I had to root for a team in this game, I'd have to pick Mae. I'm relieved she sees through him and isn't going to fall for his fake charms and cheesy one-liners like she did when they were goofy teenagers.

Yet I'm still here tonight to help my brother. From his version, things didn't go well. I'd love to hear Mae's side because I'm sure he left out a bunch of shit in order to make himself come off better. That's always been his style.

Guys like him need a pocket Cyrano de Bergerac to guide

them through interacting with women. Like Siri with less snark and better relationship advice. Something other than me groaning and telling him not to voice the shit in his head.

We share the same DNA and were raised by the same parents. Blows my mind how it's possible for two brothers to be so opposite in all but physical appearance. He's always been an asshole. At twelve, I started calling him LS. Not for Landon Samuel, but for Little Shit. Even if he's bigger than me from years of playing rugby, he'll always be my little brother.

Landon isn't the one who keeps catching my attention at this party. I couldn't care less about my brother's activities at the moment. The brunette with familiar eyes and a smile that brightens the room holds all of my attention.

Landon appears by my side, a cocktail in each hand.

I take one of the glasses and point at the mystery woman with my other hand. "Who's that?"

Following my index finger, he smirks. "Mae or the blonde woman next to her?"

Shit.

"That's Mae London? I didn't recognize her." *Shitshitshit.*

"She's super hot, right? When was the last time you saw her?" Landon doesn't take his eyes off of her.

"Twelve years ago? Maybe a few random sightings when I was home briefly, but I don't think we've spoken a word to each other since she was hanging out with you when you were in high school. She's stunning." I'm sure my voice betrays the happy surprise I'm feeling at seeing Mae again.

And then it hits me: my current mission is to help Captain Dickhead impress her. I don't know who I feel worse for: her or myself.

"Bro, don't get any ideas." He slaps me on the shoulder harder than necessary. "I called dibs on her."

Closing my eyes, I try to remember my promise to help him

out. "You can't call dibs on a person. She has a say in who she dates and isn't some sort of first come, first served donut truck."

Trailing his index finger over his bottom lip, he stares at Mae's body. "All you can eat sounds all right with me."

I close my eyes again to keep from rolling them. "Right. You seem like the giving kind of guy."

Confirming my suspicion, he laughs and slaps my shoulder again. "I'm the meal, dude."

I should walk away now. Leave him to his self-destruction. Escape any close association with him.

"Lesson one, don't be a selfish bastard. If you want a woman to go down on you, be prepared to reciprocate. Hell, do one better, be the one to initiate." I track Mae's movement through the crowd.

The black dress she's wearing hugs her curves and strong thighs. I wonder if she still snowboards competitively. I'd ask Landon, but I doubt he pays attention to the details of other people's lives enough to give me accurate information.

Instead of being a bystander to his inevitable crash and burn, I'm going to go through with my promise to make him a better man. Not for him, but for Mae. She deserves a decent guy and not dude bro Landon. If not her, then whoever he ends up with next.

God, I hope there's a next after Mae. Then maybe I'll have a shot with her.

"Let's go over and say hello," I suggest. "I want to watch you in action."

That's only part of my motivation.

"Good idea. Maybe you'll learn a few tricks, too." He straightens his back and rolls his shoulders. "Let's do this. Time to disintegrate some panties."

I groan. "Don't repeat that sentence in front of her. In fact, don't mention her clothing unless you're paying a compliment."

"Gotcha."

I duck away from his third shoulder smack. "Stop hitting me. You don't need to emphasize everything with bodily contact. Words are enough."

"You're so grumpy. How do you ever pull any women? Why am I taking your advice?"

"Fuck off. I'm helping you because you're a fucking disaster. We need a secret code if you go off the rails. If I clear my throat, stop talking. I'll step in and get you back on safer ground. Got it?"

"You have so little faith in me."

I spot Mae through a gap in the crowd. She's standing with a group of women, talking, and laughing.

"Do you know those women?" I ask Landon as we approach.

"I know all of them." He lowers his voice. "The pixie blonde is an ex. Next to her is my teammate, Lee. I went to dinner with the curly-haired blonde once. She started making out with Jesse Hayes in the middle of the meal at La Belle Femme. The fourth is Zoe and the guy standing next to her is Justin Garrison from the Easy Z Ranch."

"So you've already pissed in Mae's pool of friends?" This new information makes my challenge ten times more difficult. There's no way her friends haven't shared stories about Landon.

"Not into water sports. That's gross." He misses my metaphor.

I don't bother explaining it to him because we've reached Mae and her group. Standing behind Landon, I let him lead while I observe.

Mae's eyes flick to mine as Landon greets the group. We both share a small smile. I'm not sure if she recognizes or remembers me.

"Your body looks fucking hot in that dress," Landon tells her.

Mae's lips pull down into a frown and a line appears between her eyebrows before she recovers. "Uh, thanks."

Lee, who's clearly a rugby player from his height and thick arms, mutters under his breath, "Dude."

Inwardly, I cringe. Clearing my throat, I interrupt Landon before he can continue speaking. I decide to play coy and see if she remembers me. "I don't believe we've been introduced. I'm Aiden, Landon's older brother."

"I remember you," Mae says with a grin. "Landon mentioned you were back in town."

"Hi, Mae." My lips curl into a smile at her happy expression. "Good to see you again."

As we look at each other, the rest of the group fades away. I'm not sure if it's a second or two, or longer, that we lose ourselves in our bubble.

Landon clears his throat and nudges his elbow into my side. "Aiden's couch surfing at my place right now."

Ah, putting me in my place to make himself appear better. Classic attempt to establish himself as top dog. From Lee's straight back and wide stance, I can tell he's the group alpha. The other guy, Justin, has his own quiet confidence that doesn't demand he be the center of attention. Both men make Landon look like a yappy lap dog trying to take on a pack of wolves.

"My brother generously offered me a temporary housing option that saved me from moving home with our parents," I explain, keeping my focus on Mae.

"We ran into your mother at Twyla's shower. She seems to be doing well." Mae leaves off the part about the wedding date. "Although she didn't mention you were back in the valley."

"Probably because she was too focused on finagling a date for your brother," Sage speaks up.

"She mentioned that." I nod.

We stand in silence for a moment as I wait for Landon to comment about the date. Sage opened the door for him to say something about looking forward to it or something to break the awkward tension.

Instead, he turns to Lee and starts talking about rugby. "You going to play the last two matches so you can qualify for the Rugby Fest tournament? Or are you taking the entire season off?"

"I'm planning to play, although I'm still thinking of retiring." When he speaks, I detect an accent that's definitely not American.

"Man, you're the same age I am. Not some old guy who has to crawl out of bed every morning. Hell, Aiden's older than you," Landon rambles, managing to insult both Lee and me.

I clear my throat again. Mae and Sage exchange a loaded look.

"I need more food. Shall we go stalk the cater waiters?" Justin asks Zoe, lacing their fingers together.

"I'll join you," Mara says. "I spotted a cupcake table earlier."

At the mention of cake, Zoe's eyes widen. "Let's go before they run out."

"Us too." Sage and Lee tell me it was nice to meet me before they wander away.

Then there were three. A bicycle with an extra training wheel.

"Seriously, your tits look incredible in that dress," Landon tells Mae in a loud whisper.

Not anticipating he'd go there as soon as they're semi-alone, I choke and cough on my mouthful of beer.

"Are you okay?" Mae asks as I attempt to inhale.

Once I'm able to breathe, I mumble, "Unacceptable, dear brother."

Landon slaps my back harder than necessary to clear my airway. "He's fine. Can I get you a drink or track down a waiter with a tray of taquitos for you? Those things are sick."

Mae touches my wrist. "Aiden, do you need some water or something?"

Landon notices the contact and frowns.

Ignoring him, I focus on her. "I'm fine. Thanks."

"Told you. Let's find some tiny rolled tacos." Landon couldn't care less if I can breathe or not.

"Go on, you two. I'm going to check out the silent auction items." I clear my throat in warning to Landon to behave. He doesn't acknowledge me. "Nice to see you again, Mae."

"I'm technically working, so I should probably check in with my director. She's supposed to give a speech at some point. Don't feel any pressure to bid. Enjoy the music and the free food." Mae's dark eyes flick from me to Landon a couple of times before she walks away.

A row of tables in the rooftop lobby hold various items up for bid. I pretend to read the descriptions of time share condos and collectibles, instead of chaperoning Landon. He's a grown man and should be able to behave on his. Keyword: should.

"So you're the brother?" Picking up a pen, Sage scribbles an amount on the bid sheet for private yoga sessions.

"You're the ex-girlfriend?" I ask, glancing at her four figure bid. "Those must be some fancy yoga classes."

"It's my donation. I want to make sure some cheapskate doesn't win."

"You bid over a grand on your own item?" I can't decide if she's brilliant or a fool.

She nods, happily. "Whips the competition into a frenzy if they think something's a hot ticket. Trust me. I'm a pro at these things."

"Professional bid rigger at charity events?" I like her. She has spirit.

"If I'm the top bidder, I'll pay. Everyone wins. Except the people who were too cheap to outbid me. They're still losers.

Gotta be all in if you want to finish first." She pins me with her gray eyes.

Changing my mind, I decide she scares me a little. "You dated my brother? Have to say I don't really see it."

"I was going through a phase. We all make decisions we regret." She shrugs off the memory. "He isn't all bad. As you probably know."

"Somedays I'm not sure." I laugh it off.

"Then why are you helping him impress Mae?" She focuses on the bid sheet for a time share in the Bahamas.

"Who said I was?" *Deny, deny, deny.*

Her eyes meet mine again and she studies me.

Uncomfortable under her scrutiny, I give her a vague answer. "Think of it as doing something for the greater good. Landon being less of an asshat benefits all of us."

Slowly, she nods, not breaking eye contact. "True. You think it's possible? Others have given him the benefit of the doubt before and had it blow up in their faces."

She points at herself.

"Better to try and fail than never get into the game, right?" I tap the bid sheet.

"I'm curious about your end game," she whispers.

"Me too," I tell her in a low voice. "The outcome is still unclear."

SEVEN

MAE

WAITING AT A traffic light, I pull out my phone and check text messages. I have two from Sage, one asking if I want to meet for lunch at the vegan place she loves, and one that is only a pic of the tops of boobs in her yoga tank. Something tells me the second text isn't intended for me. I hit reply and snap a pic of my own cleavage to return the favor.

Immediately, she responds with the horrified emoji scream face and then two apples and heart eyes. Laughing at her message, I add a bikini and flames to my response. We could communicate only in emojis all day, every day, and never stop being amused.

Crossing the street, I wonder if there will be a return to hieroglyphics instead of bothering to type words.

My phone pings with a new text. It's Landon.

Yes, I saved him into my contacts and that's as far as our commitment is going.

I open his text and read it.

Great to see you last night. You looked beautiful.

His words catch me off guard and I trip, but stop myself before I face-plant.

His words are polite, respectable, and flattering in an appropriate way.

Bouncing dots appear on the left side of the screen, indicating he's still typing. I wait for a comment about my boobs or ass. This is Landon, after all.

I apologize if any of my comments came off as rude. Working on my brain to mouth filter.

A compliment and an apology is a whole new level of weird coming from the king of inappropriate.

Thanks. I use the whole word to be more formal. I'm about to type "new phone, who dis" when another text appears.

It's Landon, btw. In case you didn't save my number. You should do that to avoid confusion.

Now he's a mind reader, too?

Someone jostles my shoulder and I realize I'm frozen in the middle of the sidewalk, staring down at my phone.

"Sorry," I apologize to no one. Glancing up, I get my bearings, suddenly feeling like I've stepped through a worm hole into another dimension. The Hotel Jerome's brick façade anchors the block ahead of me. Is nine-thirty too early for an adult beverage when not on vacation? Asking for a friend.

Probably not my best idea to show up to my volunteer job with mimosa or Bloody Mary breath. Not if I want to eventually get a paid position at a local non-profit if I stay in the area.

I know it's you. Afraid he'll read too much into it, I hate admitting I've already saved his number.

What are you doing up so early?

What does he think I do when I'm not working? Loaf around? Work on my tan at the pool? Sleep 'til noon?

On my way to work.

At the La Belle Femme?

At Coalition. Are you surprised I'm one of those good doers and not just a pretty face?

He responds instantly. *Never thought you were just one thing. Doesn't surprise me you're both beautiful and passionate.*

I wait for the sex joke. When it doesn't come, I try to think of something snarky to bite back with, but I'm thrown off by his nice compliments. Could it be possible I saved the wrong number as Landon?

I wish we had more time to talk last night. What are you doing this weekend?

Bridezilla festivities.

All weekend? He adds a sad face to his message.

Pretty much.

Too bad.

Why?

I want to catch up with you. Hear more about your work.

Never once has Landon asked me about anything of substance. He said he'd try, and maybe this is him putting in effort not to be a human crotch rocket—fast and flashy.

I side-eye my screen. *Why are you being so nice?*

Do I need a reason? Fine. It's Monday. The sun's out. I'm only pointing out the truth.

Prove you're Landon. Show me proof. He might be charming, but I'm not going to let my guard down around him.

Wait, that didn't come out right. He isn't going to send me a dick pic, is he?

I quickly close the text window out of fear. Another notification appears on my home screen and I peer at it with one eye closed in case it contains a tiny thumbnail of Landon's dick. Relief floods my chest when I only see emojis.

Opening Sage's response, I laugh at her invitation to tacos and margaritas with a thumb's down on eggplant, aka penises. Tomorrow is Taco Tuesday and she's crazy if she thinks I'm going to miss our weekly girls' night. With everyone mated off, taco night is sacred friendship time. This week we seriously need to debrief about the charity event, Aiden's reappearance, and what I'm going to do about my crazy family wedding.

Landon sends another text and I swipe up to ignore the notification.

Scrolling through emojis, I click on the taco, thumb's up, lipstick, the eggplant, and the see no evil monkey before hitting send.

Texting while walking is distracting, and before I know, I'm standing outside of the Coalition's office space. I tuck my phone into my bag and smooth a hand over my braided bun. If I'm going to stay in Aspen, I need to make a good impression in order to network my way into a job that doesn't involve Nutella and grabby handed male customers.

Wow, I sound like a stripper. Not that there's anything wrong with dancing for money. I'd earn more in tips if I were topless. Imagining how appalled my mother would be at me, I giggle. I guess I still have some of my rebellious streak.

Inside of the office, I greet Carmen who is both office manager and mother figure in the office for the tiny five-person staff, six including me. With her short salt and pepper hair, she's no nonsense and not afraid to use her mom voice if needed, even when dealing with people older than she is.

"Who was that handsome man you were talking to last night?" she asks while I get settled at my small desk near the window.

I sling my bag over a hook next to my work station, remove my phone from inside of it, and then pull out my chair. "Which one? I'm friends with a bunch of the rugby guys, but not all of them are good looking. What color hair?"

"Light brown, dark blond hair. So rugged and handsome," she purrs. "I could probably be his mother, but I'm not blind. Please tell me you're sleeping with him and he's as gorgeous naked as he is clothed."

Sweet lord. I should've had the morning cocktail. My iced latte is not going to get me through this morning if Carmen transforms into rugby fan girl.

"Landon Roberts. Big guy? He's one of the rugby players. Do you ever go to the matches at Wagner Park? You should. If you like watching men in shorts running and tackling and going all full contact on each other while grunting and sweating." I think I've also described gay porn and hope she doesn't come to the same conclusion.

"No, no. I know the players. I haven't missed a Rugby Fest in twenty-five years. The whole weekend is blocked off on my calendar. I can't wait." She points at the wall calendar behind her, and sure enough, two weeks from now has a big red circle drawn around the weekend. "The man I'm talking about had a beard. Ring a bell? I'm hoping he's a late season recruit for the club. Do you have the scoop on him?"

Underneath her neatly trimmed hair, organic cotton clothes, and shoes made from recycled plastic bottles lies a woman who could probably make Landon and Easley blush.

"Bearded rugby player?" I'm stumped.

"White shirt. Jeans that hugged his ass like a lover's hands." She makes a cupping and squeezing motion with her own hands.

I feel my eyes bug out. "Aiden? Looks like he might have a squirrel's nest hidden in his facial hair?"

"Nice name. I like my men a little bit feral. Keeps things interesting." Her purr is back and she has a glimmer in her eyes.

I'm seeing a whole new side to Carmen this morning. Part of me wants to give her a high-five, but the bigger part wants to never speak of her lust for Aiden Roberts again.

She can have Landon. I'll happily make the introductions.

"Sorry to pop your bubble, but Aiden's not a player." At least not on the rugby pitch. "More of fixer upper, complete rehab project."

Her face falls into a frown. "I didn't get that vibe from him at all."

"Oh, don't get me wrong, he's a good guy. Having a little rough patch. Hopefully he'll figure things out and get back on his feet soon."

I don't want to gossip about him to Carmen. That's how rumors are started. I tell her, she tells a friend, they tell two friends . . . and with each new person the story will change and grow. Not fair to Aiden.

"Interesting. Avery and I were going over the winning bids from the auction, and someone with the last name Roberts made a sizable donation by being the top bidder on three of the donated items." She opens a folder. "At least I think the name was Aiden. Now I'm wondering if it was Landon."

"I seriously doubt it was Aiden. You didn't take a check from him, did you? It might bounce." I cover my mouth with my hand. Seeing Carmen's horrified expression, I add, "Ha ha. I'm joking."

"Defrauding a charity isn't a laughing matter." Shuffling through the stack of bid sheets, she pulls out a group paper-clipped together. "Aha! I knew I remembered the name. Aiden Roberts."

My morning coffee churns in my stomach. Why would he bid if he's broke? "How much did he donate?"

"Thirty-one hundred. Certainly not the evening's biggest donor, but enough that he caught Avery's attention." She pulls off the clip holding the bid sheets together.

Avery is our director of fundraising. A wealthy divorcée who got the ski house in her divorce settlement and decided to move here full time, she's a master of getting money out of wealthy people, especially men. I don't remember seeing her chatting with Aiden last night, but I was pretty busy doing my ninja maneuvers to avoid Landon.

"What did he win?" I stand on my toes so I can peer over her desk to read better.

Flapping the pages at me, she wards off my attempt. "Thought you said it was impossible for him to have bid and paid?"

This is worse than I imagined. "Did he pay by credit card or check?"

"Who carries checks around anymore? He paid by credit card, which was approved. I don't know why you're so concerned about this. Bid and bought. Done deal." Casting a doubtful look at me, she slips the clip around the pages and hands them to me.

Silently, I ask what Aiden was thinking. Maybe he was trying to impress his brother or show him up. The two of them can be competitive, or at least they were growing up. Whatever Aiden could do, Landon had to do it better. The memory brings up a new theory.

"Did Landon win any items?" Perhaps Aiden bid to raise his brother's bids and then got stuck as the top bidder. If he isn't familiar with these kind of events, he wouldn't know that he could cancel before paying.

"No, I don't see his name." She closes the folder, patiently waiting for me to hand back the papers I'm holding.

"Hmm," I hum out loud. "What have you done, Aiden?"

"Bought himself a balloon ride for two, four private yoga classes, and a night in a suite and a tasting menu dinner at the chef's table at the Jerome. Not only is he hot in a feral way, he's also a romantic and has a girlfriend. Lucky lady." Carmen sighs.

I stare at the paper in my hand like some secret code or message in invisible ink will reveal the motivation behind Aiden's actions. Girlfriend? Carmen has a point about him being handsome and he is the nicer of the two brothers, which isn't saying a whole lot, but beyond those two points, he isn't exactly a catch.

Are women so desperate these days that a nice ass, incredible abs—I assume based on the amount of muscles in his arms and shoulders—and a halfway decent personality are the best we can expect from men?

What happened to having a good job and a plan for the future? I'm not talking boring, conservative guys like Zoe's ex who never want to get their heart rate elevated off of the slopes. There must be a happy zone between slacker and up-tight overachiever.

Still confused, I hand back the papers and take the few steps to my desk. I specifically told him he didn't have to feel pressure to bid. Now he's out three grand for a balloon ride and some yoga classes.

"Hold on, those yoga sessions. Were they with Sage Blum?" I turn to face Carmen.

"She's the only one who donated yoga, so yes." Carmen gives me a funny look and then focuses on her computer. "None of my business, but you seem overly concerned about this man."

"Trying to watch out for an old friend." Not exactly the truth, but better than telling her about the gambling and hookers. *Alleged* gambling and hookers and rare rap albums.

A new theory about Aiden's wasted millions crystalizes. What if he spent all of his money on random shit at charity auctions?

Needing to share this twist of events with the girls, I pull out my phone to send a group text. Another notification from Landon as well as a new text alert from Sage fill the home screen.

Landon's text catches my eye because it's a combination of eggplant, cherries, and a row of peaches.

"Okay. That's weird," I say to myself, clicking open the full message.

That's when I see my last text to him.

Taco, thumbs-up, lipstick, and eggplant followed by three

see no evil monkeys.

"No, fucking way," I say softly, but not quietly enough.

"Language. This is a professional office," Carmen chastises me like I'm a wild biker let loose in the pristine white, modern office with tasteful natural wood accents and succulents on every desk.

"Sorry. I just received shocking news." If she only knew how shocking.

I think I just proposed sex with Landon using emojis.

Not sure what role the monkey plays in my bizarre scenario. Landon's clearly open to the idea. Or he's on a weird eggplant and fruit vegan diet.

"Are eggplants fruit?" I ask Carmen.

She sighs. "In fact, they are. You're having a very Monday Monday, aren't you? I don't know if you need more caffeine or less."

"Thanks. More coffee is always the answer." I notice we're the only two people in the office this morning. "Where is everyone?"

"It's Monday. Staff meeting." She throws some major shade in my direction. "You might want to get that second cup of coffee before you begin working."

I'm off my game because of some random eggplant. This isn't a big deal.

Picking up my phone, I walk over to the small kitchen to make myself a coffee. I forward a screenshot of my text and Landon's response to the group, explaining the first text was for Sage.

Me: *Did I sext Landon by mistake?!!!*

Sage responds with ten horrified faces. Mara sends five laughing-crying emojis. Zoe must not be by her phone because I don't receive an immediate response.

Mara: *At least you didn't send that text to your mother.*

Me: *Like Margaret knows eggplant equals dick. She'd think it was a pictogram of my grocery list.*

Sage: *I wonder what he thinks the monkey means.*

Zoe: *Kinky, blindfolded monkey. And wow, he jumped from blowjobs to butt stuff in one text.*

I groan because she's right. All those peaches. So disappointing. We'd been having a nice chat using words before I turned the conversation pervy.

Sage responds with more horrified scream faces.

Zoe: *Sorry, Sage. I keep forgetting you dated him.*

Me: *What should I do?* I pour some milk into my coffee, changing the black liquid to a light caramel.

Sage: *Burn your phone and get a new number?*

Mara: *Block him?*

Zoe: *See how far you can push him?* Zoe adds a banana, a shark, and a grinning face.

Sage: *Gross.*

Mara: *I don't get it.*

Zoe: *Period sex.*

Mara: *That escalated quickly.*

Me: *Exactly my point.*

Zoe: *Fine. Text him back and say you sent it to the wrong person.*

Sage: *Genius. Will make him think you already have a man so he'll back off.*

Me: *If I had a man, I wouldn't need a wedding date.*

Zoe: *Want me to find you a cowboy on the ranch? I can't promise he won't smell like horses.*

I laugh at her suggestion. *Wouldn't hurt to look.*

Zoe: *Done and done.*

Voices carry from the hall, indicating the staff meeting is over.

Me: *Gotta go*

Mara: *Me too. These cat testicles won't remove themselves. :-)*

Sage: *So gross.*

I love my friends, but this morning has been a strange one.

Thankfully, there are no more sexts from Landon for the rest of the morning. Maybe my silence is response enough to keep him from responding.

EIGHT

MAE

"DON'T LOOK, BUT I think Twyla is here." Sage nudges my foot with hers.

Ignoring her command, I glance over my shoulder. Sure enough my cousin is perched on a bar stool. "Who's she with? I can't see around the pillar for a clear view without moving."

Zoe leans to the right. "Topher. I think."

"I should go over and say hello. The spirit of my mother is poking me in the ribs to be polite," I grumble, lamely attempting to hoist myself out of my chair. "Too many tacos. Can't do it."

"You don't have to get up. They're coming our way." Mara straightens in her seat like the queen is approaching. Her perfect posture would make my mother proud.

I won't tell her she has a tiny fragment of tortilla chip stuck in one of her curls until after my cousin leaves.

"Hi, Mae," Twyla chirps like a happy little bird. "It's so nice to run into you."

Giving her the courtesy of my full attention, I twist in my chair to face her. I seriously don't think I could stand right now.

"Hi, and hi to Topher, too." I stumble over the to-Topher-too combination. "Excited for the big day?"

He nods, completely emotionless.

"We're both excited about our weekend trips. I hope you can all make my bachelorette weekend." She grins at our group. "Even if you originally RSVP'd no, you can still join. We have open spots for the rafting trip on Saturday and the spa day on Sunday, too. A few girls had to cancel last minute."

"That's so sweet of you." Sage flashes her a bright smile. "Unfortunately, I won't be able to make it because it's the last rugby game of the season and Lee will be playing. Thank you."

Mara has a horrified expression on her face. "I, I won't be free on Saturday either. We're expecting an arrival of new dogs from a shelter in Denver. I have to be there to, ah . . . check them in. Can I still join the spa day?"

Twyla nods. "Of course. Zoe and Mae? Still joining us?"

My cousin's smile wavers for a second before she slips it back into place. I know I can't skip the weekend or I'll never hear the end of it at every family gathering about how I didn't support and celebrate her wedding enough.

I give her a half-hearted thumbs-up. "I'll be there. What time?"

"We're meeting at 7:30 a.m. in Aspen. You can stumble out of bed. No need to do your hair or makeup because we plan on getting wet and wild!" Her enthusiasm reminds me of a bubbly, blond cheerleader.

Seems early for day drinking by the pool while having spa treatments, but I don't question it further. Nor do I challenge her idea of wild. She probably means mismatching the colors of her manicure and pedicure. Going with the flow and being delightful are my two goals for surviving this weekend.

"Sounds like fun!" I flash my teeth at her in a hopefully friendly and excited grin.

"Fewer teeth and less hungry looking," Sage whispers behind her hand.

Her warning makes me laugh, which is genuine.

"We're going to have the best time." Zoe nods and lifts her glass in a toast. "Can't wait."

Topher curves his lips into a closed mouth smile. In combination with his vaguely pained expression, he could be getting a prostate exam inside of his expensive plaid shorts. "Sounds more fun than what we're doing."

I believe him.

"What are the guys doing? Strippers and weed in Denver?"

If I were drinking something, I'd do a spit take at Zoe's question.

"We are going to Denver for a baseball game and a couple rounds of golf," he answers her like she asked a normal question. Have to give it to him, he's unflappable. Too rich to care about silly jokes.

Twyla's smile widens and she tucks her head against his shoulder. "I love that they're not doing a Vegas bachelor weekend. So cliché."

My eyes meet Sage's.

"Right. Of course. Smart." Mara nods in approval. "Who needs all that fake glamor and temptation for debauchery in their lives? Not me."

Thankfully, Topher and Twyla say their goodbyes, and then leave.

"I can't with him." Zoe finishes her margarita and then licks the salted sugar rim. "Reminds me way too much of the life I almost led."

"He's from a very good family," I offer in defense. "They're a perfect match. Except for their names. My tongue gets all twisted trying to say Topher and Twyla Tierney."

We all try saying it as fast as we can, ending up in a pile of giggles. Laughing so hard I almost slip out of my chair, I wipe the gathering tears in the corners of my eyes.

Once she regains her ability to breathe, Zoe asks, "Are you excited to go white water rafting?"

"No. Why would I go rafting in ice cold snow run-off? That's for tourists and river rats." I frown at her like she's gone full crazy-pants. "Are you going rafting?"

My friends go quiet and stare at me.

"Were you paying attention to Twyla?" Mara asks.

"Did you read the invitation for the bachelorette weekend or the weekly email updates?" Sage dips her chin so she can give me her serious face.

"I only ever half listen to her. If she isn't talking about her wedding, she's reliving her glory days in the athletes' village at Sochi. I could repeat multiple stories on both subjects from memory. My mother said yes on my behalf to any and all events surrounding this circus."

"There are no new animals arriving at the ranch this week-end." Mara gives me a sharp look. "I made that up to avoid going whitewater rafting with Twyla and her friends. Even with a helmet and the appropriate safety gear, me in a kayak is a disaster waiting to happen."

"Okay, you stressed me out that I missed the memo." Sage sighs with relief. She's on the board and volunteers at Hawks' Ranch where Mara's the veterinarian. "That was clever."

"Thanks. Good thing you had the rugby match to fall back on. Lucky that." Mara holds her fist out for a bump.

Sage bumps her hand. "Not sure if Lee's going to play. He's being weird about playing since he broke his leg last year. In any case, we'll go to the match to cheer on the club."

"Hold the front door." I point at each of them in turn. "My stuffy cousin is forcing us to go rafting together. And you let me agree to this while you all had outs? You're leaving me on my own with the bride and her merry band of boring bridesmaids?"

"Hey, what about me?" Zoe asks. "I'm excited to go. Never

been and I've lived here for years."

I ignore her because she isn't helping my cause, which at the moment is outrage. "Why didn't anyone warn me? I could've made up an excuse about work. Or getting a root canal." Oh, I should save that one for the wedding. Emergency root canal would be a solid reason to miss the blessed event.

"Do you ever check your emails?" Mara asks.

"On my phone. But if they're too long, I skim and tell myself I'll read them later, which of course I never do." This turn of events has ruined my happy taco night.

"You have no one to blame but yourself," Sage tells me bluntly. "Like the Landon date. I think this is the universe telling you to stand up for yourself and to stop being a people pleaser with your family."

I scowl at her. "Way to harsh my buzz."

"Hold on, I think I've found a silver lining," Mara pipes up.

"Does it involve a note from a questionable doctor? You're a doctor, can you write me an excuse? Say I have kennel cough or an ear infection. I trust you to come up with something believable."

Zoe snorts from across the table. "It's going to be fun. We're not going in the big rafts. Everyone will get their own kayak. You can paddle away from anyone who annoys you. Bonus, there could be cute guides."

I like her points, except individual kayaks. Sounds like a lot of work.

"That was my silver lining," Mara exclaims, her curls bouncing as she claps her hands. "Doesn't Aiden work as a rafting guide?"

"He does," I say warily. "However, there's more than one rafting operation in the valley. I don't know which one he works for or which company Twyla hired for her shindig."

"Trust the universe," Sage tells me, sounding all namaste,

zen, earth goddess.

"My luck isn't that good. Or bad." I'm not sure spending time with Aiden is a good idea.

"We'll find out bright and early Saturday morning. The weather's supposed to be gorgeous and warm. I think it's going to be a great adventure." Zoe's undeterred by my disinterest.

Easy for her to say.

I try to find a bright spot. Carmen's words about Aiden's abs float back through my head.

If his shirt gets wet, he'll probably take it off at some point. Getting a glimpse of his fine body would be a nice side bonus of the day. And I could report back to Carmen with confirmation. If I'm sneaky I could even snap a pic for her.

"I need more coffee." I sip from the stainless steel travel mug in my hand.

"You're drinking coffee right now. Or did you put something else in there today?" She leans closer to sniff my mug.

"I worked last night and got up at six-thirty. Let's stop at the bakery for snacks and more coffee." I sling my backpack higher on my shoulder. "We have time if we don't dawdle on the corner."

Zoe laughs. "Remember earlier this summer when you went all Julie Andrews on me and made me climb all the mountains?"

"I do. You should be grateful I didn't make you sing." I pick up my pace as the bakery comes into view.

"That was one of the best days of my life." She catches up and walks beside me. "Thank you."

"Uh, you're welcome. Why are you feeling nostalgic? No mountains will be climbed today." I can smell the baked goods from across the street, and cut diagonally across the corner to get there sooner.

"I'm hoping today's one of the best days of your life, too."

Opening the screen door, I step through just as a baker carries a tray of fresh croissants and pan au chocolat to the display case.

"I think it could possibly be a very good day," I tell Zoe before ordering enough buttery pastry for the entire group. Not that I plan to share the whole dozen, but I will if pushed.

Fresh coffees and breakfast acquired, we still have time for a quick pee in the bakery's restroom, perhaps our last proper toilet access for hours, before walking to meet the group.

The vans and trailers full of kayaks are parked in a row up ahead, and I immediately begin scanning for a familiar mop of brown hair and a beard that resembles an otter hugging a man's neck. Piles of overnight bags are stacked on the curb and I feel like I under packed. I spot Twyla standing in a group of women. She's hard to miss, dressed all in white and pink, and wearing a tiara with a veil. I return her enthusiastic wave and grin.

"This should be interesting," Zoe says softly beside me. "At the very least it will make a good story we can tell for many years to come."

"If we don't die," I add as we cross the street to join the rest of the ladies.

"No one is going to die." Aiden steps from behind me. "Not on my watch."

Welp, I guess that answers the big question of the day.

He's dressed in what I assume is the finest in rafting guide clothing. He's wearing a T-shirt that clings to his shoulders and pecs, along with cargo shorts in a material that screams wicking and water resistance. Chacos cover his feet. A black fabric cord loops around his neck and secures his classic black Wayfarers. Even with the sun-bleached, faded navy baseball cap, I would be able to pick him out of a lineup of other guides.

"Were you following us?" I lead with an accusation to distract him from my staring.

"Only from the corner. I ran over to Clarks for some lip balm."

"Planning to be doing some kissing today?" I ask.

"You never know, but I needed it for the sun protection. We're at high altitude and will be on the water. Recipe for sun damage." He holds out a new tube of balm. "You can borrow some if you need it."

"I have a whole kit of stuff in my bag." I pat one of my shoulder straps. "But thank you."

There are better ways to share lip balm than sharing the same tube.

Now I'm thinking about kissing his full lips. That's when I notice his beard isn't nearly so swamp dweller and much more neater.

"You trimmed your beard?" I ask without thinking.

"I did. You like it?" He strokes the remaining beard that no longer hangs past his chin like Spanish moss off of a tree branch.

"Much better. Although you might want to put away the lip balm around this group," I caution him while subtly pointing to Twyla and her acolytes. "Wedding fever. It's contagious when unmarried women of a certain age are around a bride. Turns level-headed, rational, kind women into raving lunatics, solely focused on getting a ring on their own finger, come hell," I pause for dramatic effect before saying with a straight face, "or high water."

His eyes are wide with disbelief, or horror—it's hard to tell. I stare up at him, keeping my face as serious as possible.

He tips his head back and laughs. "Nice pun on the high water."

That's it? I've warned him of a potential mauling today and he laughs at my pun ability?

"Okay, everybody," he says to the group, raising his voice

loud enough to be heard over the chattering, "listen up.

"I'm Aiden and I'll be your leader today. I have Mitch with me as a secondary guide and photographer. And last but not least, meet Steve, who is our hospitality and safety liaison. He'll be in the big raft with our food and supplies. Anyone who needs a snack or a Band-aid on the river, Steve will take care of you."

"Will he kiss it and make it better?" a petite and curvy red-head asks, causing the other women to giggle.

Aiden twists his head to face me. "See?" I mouth at him in a triumphant told you so moment.

A small, baby smile curls his full lips before he continues speaking. "The plan is to drive down valley to our launch area. After a short training session, we'll put out boats in the river and get acclimated before paddling together as a group so we can guide you through the rapids. Today's run has class two and class three white water, but there will also be stretches of calm water. Be prepared. You're definitely going to get wet."

This earns more giggles from all the women present and Mitch.

Poor Aiden.

"What's that Kevin Bacon rafting movie? With the family and evil Bacon?" Zoe whispers into my ear.

"*River Wild*," I whisper back. "I think Aiden could be played by a young Kevin."

Aiden chuckles. There's zero chance he heard her, but I think he's finally catching on to the vibe of today's group. I doubt we're the first group of women he's had to deal with, but we might be the worst.

"What if we've never gone rafting before?" Zoe asks, and several women nod in agreement.

"You should be fine. If anyone decides being in a kayak isn't for them, you can ride with Steve. I'm sure he'll be happy to have you join him." Aiden pats Steve's shoulder like the poor guy has pulled the short straw.

I giggle and cover it with my hand, pretending to stifle a yawn, which then turns into a real yawn because it's too damn early to be an attentive listener.

"Everyone should've filled out the release of liability form. If you didn't, or you forgot it at home, or the dog ate it, I have more here. Grab one if you need it." He points to the ground where the forms poke out of a plastic bin. "Once we have your paperwork, feel free to get in one of the vans."

Zoe steps forward to grab two. "I know you forgot."

I accept it because she's right, but I still stick my tongue out at her. I'd flip her off if both my hands weren't full of coffee and the bag of pastries.

"Anyone need a pen?" Aiden holds up a handful of ballpoints and faces me.

It's like he knows me so well already.

Forced to put my coffee and pastries down, I accept a pen from him.

"Here, you can use my back as a clipboard." He steps in front of me and rolls his shoulders forward to flatten his back. No big deal.

I gently smooth out the wrinkles of his T-shirt. The cotton is super soft under my fingers and thin enough I can feel the warmth of his skin underneath the fabric. He smells of laundry detergent and sunscreen, clean and fresh. Beneath my hand his muscles bunch and ripple over his ribs. The man is ripped—not in the big, bulging biceps and giant quads way like his brother, but in a sleek, fast way of a mountain lion.

Sweet heavens above. I'm comparing him to the cousin of the king of the jungle. Snapping out of my haze, I realize I'm now touching him with both hands. One presses the paper flat and the other is resting on his waist. Why? For balance? His or mine?

My worst fear is realized when he twists his head to stare at me. "Doesn't the pen work?"

Zoe snorts from somewhere to my left. I can't look at her right now or I'll turn bright red.

He must know I haven't tried to write anything because the hand holding the pen is on his waist and he can probably see it if he glances down.

"I, uh," I stutter as I try to come up with a reason I haven't filled out the short form. "I forgot my address. Brain freeze."

Wanting to die or at least run down the street away from him, I quickly scribble out my name, address, and phone number before signing the form.

"There you go. All signed." I hand him the paper. "You're in charge of my life now. If I should die today, know I don't hold a grudge."

Zoe hands him her paperwork, too. "We're all set. Thanks."

I can't even look at Aiden as I tug Zoe over to the van.

"What's wrong with you?" she whispers as she climbs inside.

"Mae?" Aiden interrupts her.

I'm on the first step, bent forward at the waist with my head ducked to avoid slamming it on the door opening. My ass is hanging out of the van, right near where Aiden is now standing. Essentially it's right in his face. Fantastic.

"Yes?" I step down so I'm no longer mooning him.

"You forgot your coffee." With a smile, he hands me my cup, his fingers brushing over mine. "No coffee or kayaker left behind."

"Uh, thanks." I stare at my hand where his fingers touch mine for a second longer before he pulls back.

"You're welcome." He steps away. "Okay, load 'em up, people. We're burning daylight. Sooner we're on the road, the sooner we'll get in the water."

With only eleven total in our group, we have room to spread

out between the two vans. Twyla comes over and declares herself the co-pilot, taking the seat up front. A couple of her friends I recognize from the bridal shower, Amy and Amanda slip past us to the back row.

Zoe and I claim the middle seat. I still can't look at her because I know she knows I'm being ridiculous over Aiden.

Instead, I open the bag from the bakery. The scent of butter and sugar fills the van.

My phone pings with a new text. From Landon. I twist in my seat so my phone is toward the window. I don't want Zoe to know I've been texting with him. She'll have me committed.

Hope you have a great day on the river.

That's nice.

Thanks. You too.

Next weekend's Rugby Fest. Come cheer me on. He adds a bicep, a trophy, and the clapping hand emojis.

Okay, a little focused on him but it's nice he's inviting me. And he didn't use an eggplant again. Hopefully he forgot about the accidental sexting.

I'll be there.

Excellent. Be sure to send me a pic of you and Twyla in your bikinis. I'm stuck at the gym all the day and need motivation.

For what? Wanking in the locker room? Oh, Landon. Every time you're ahead, you go and ruin it.

I decide to ignore his last text and pretend I forgot to respond.

Aiden climbs into the driver's seat and closes his door. He turns in his seat to face the back. "What smells so good?"

"I have pastries," I tell him. "Croissants. Pan au chocolat. Almond croissants."

"You brought an entire selection of French baked goods with you?" His smile widens when he stares at me. I can't see his eyes through his sunglasses but I'm sure they're amused.

"Seemed appropriate. Want some? I bought enough to

share." I hold out the bag to him.

"I'm good, thanks," he says, laughing.

"I'll have one. I probably shouldn't because I need to fit into my wedding dress, but they smell so good." Twyla takes the bag from my hand.

Everyone but Aiden munches on pastry as we drive out of town. Even though his sunglasses block his eyes, I swear he keeps glancing at me in the rearview mirror. Then again I'm sitting right behind him and he's probably checking on the trailer behind us. That makes more sense.

NINE

MAE

STRIPPING OFF MY leggings, I hop around on the rocky shore in a demonstration of grace and balance. Reluctantly, I slip off my sweatshirt. In just my rash guard and bikini bottom, goose bumps cover my cold skin and my nipples tighten into small buds. Glancing around, I see I'm not the only one nipping out in my bathing suit. We're all Team Nipple. I hope the padding of my vest creates some warmth. There's no way the water isn't icy cold.

Helmet on, vest strapped closed, sunglasses secured, and my water booties covering my feet, I'm finally ready.

"Should we do a group before pic?" Twyla suggest. "While we all still look hot?"

Speaking of hot, Aiden is shirtless under his vest. I missed the moment of seeing his bare chest when he changed. Sadly, it's for the best. I can't spend all day ogling him. For many reasons including his questionable life decisions. The worst being is he's Landon's brother.

I glance at the other two men among us. Mitch is all bare chested and tan, but I swear he's like nineteen, twenty at most. Steve still sports his shirt under his vest and looks like he's in his forties or fifties. Maybe it's because he's wearing a canvas hat with a chin strap like my dad would.

Too young. Too old. Just right but not mine.

I'm Goldilocks.

Not that this matters because nothing is going to happen with any of them. Not today. Or any day.

We huddle into a clump around Twyla. Mitch holds out his GoPro on a stick to take the pic.

Aiden goes over some safety information while we're still on land. Holding our paddles, we practice our strokes before getting into our inflatable kayaks, aka the duckies. Guess this makes Aiden our momma duck.

This spot on the river has a calm pool to one side, which allows us a place to practice paddling before being carried away by the current to roaring rapids.

No one capsizes or fails the basics, so Aiden declares us good to go.

Zoe and I stick together near the front of the group. The first stretch of river is pretty low key and we all paddle along like happy ducklings, chatting and laughing at random things. So far we've had small sections of choppy white water but no major challenges.

"This is nice," I tell Zoe. The sun's warmed up my skin to the point where the occasional splash of water feels refreshing. The banks flanking the river stretch high above us as we enter a canyon.

Aiden and Mitch have been trading off between being at the front of the pack and the back, checking in on us and giving tips. Ahead of the kayaks, Steve handles the larger raft on his own, sitting on the back edge, holding a large paddle in each hand. According to Aiden, Steve will go ahead and get lunch set up for us.

"Glad you're enjoying yourself. We're about to hit our first set of class three rapids," Aiden shouts so the entire group can hear him.

"What happened to class two? Shouldn't we ease ourselves into this?" I glance around us to see if anyone else thinks this is a bait and switch.

"You've already gone through three sections of those. Follow me and you'll be fine. If you capsize, get your feet facing down river as quickly as possible, and enjoy the ride." Aiden grins at us, before paddling ahead.

"If I capsize? Don't you mean when?" I ask nervously while frantically paddling to keep up with him.

Blocked by a curve in the river, I can't see the impending rapids, but I can hear the roar of water.

I glance around to see if anyone else is worried about what lies ahead. Spotting Zoe slightly behind me, I twist to face her. "You okay?"

"Ask me in about five minutes." She smiles, but her shoulders are tense.

"Face front, Mae," Aiden shouts at me. "Rule number one, don't hit a rapid going sideways."

Hearing the urgency in his voice, I pay attention to what's coming.

My kayak bumps and dips through the water as I'm sucked forward in the speeding current. Aiden navigates boulders and small drops with ease. Meanwhile, I'm frantically paddling from side to side, desperately trying to follow his path through this watery hell-scape.

"Oh shit," I scream as the water begins churning around us. Ahead, mist rises in the air and roaring drowns out any other noise.

"No turning back. Here we go!" His enthusiasm fails to comfort me.

Somewhere behind me someone else screams. It's a woman, or Mitch has too much icy water near his balls.

Water churns in every direction and I fight to keep the nose of my kayak pointing downstream. I'm being tossed around like a leaf in a hot tub with the jets at full blast. My head feels like someone is shaking it while giving me a tequila shooter.

A gigantic, tsunami-size wave crashes over me and everything goes watery for a few seconds until I pop back up and see the sky again.

"Waterfall straight ahead!" Mitch or Aiden or God's voice carries over the roar.

We're going *over* a waterfall? That sounds like something only crazy people try to do at Niagara Falls.

When Aiden disappears over the drop, I realize it's too late to reverse this terrible decision

Approaching the falls, I flex my feet under the safety strap and hold my paddle in a death grip. Even I know the expression up a creek without a paddle is a bad thing.

The next few seconds are a blur of white water, fear, and the certainty this is how I'm going to die.

At the bottom of the falls sits a wide pool of frothy water. I get stuck in an eddy for a moment, too stunned by recent events to remember how to get myself out.

"Out of the way, Mae. Or Zoe's going to land on your head." Aiden's voice carries over to me from the side.

I quickly paddle to where he's floating in a calm spot of water and wait for the others to join us.

"How was it?" he asks, grinning as if he's just had the best sex of his life.

Adrenaline makes my heart thrash around in my chest like it's dancing to speed metal. I'm breathless, too.

"I'll let you know when I'm on solid, dry, not moving land again."

His smile widens even more. "Good thing our lunch spot is close."

"Aye chihuahua!" I scream when my foot slips and the water

splashes up to my crotch. "It's freezing!"

Aiden appears beside me, his warm hand on my elbow. With a chuckle and a slight tone of sarcasm, he tells me, "It's snow runoff, you know."

If he weren't a giant mountain of a man, I'd attempt to shove him into the river and see how much his delicate balls like the frigid temperature. He'd probably scream like a tiny baby. Instead, I allow him to help me navigate the few steps to dry land.

Without shame, I flop on the sun warmed rocks and lie back, gratefully scraping my hands over the rocks and gritty sand. A shadow blocks my sun for a second before I feel someone sit next to me. Peeling one eye open, I tip my head to spot Zoe beside me.

"That was crazy. I feel like someone's pumped me full of caffeine and sugar, and then sent me on the craziest log ride slash rollercoaster ever." All of her teeth flash with her wide grin. "I can't wait to hit more rapids."

"You're high on the adrenaline." I poke her shoulder with my index finger.

"I am. We should go sky diving after this. Or maybe para-sailing. This is more fun than skiing."

I wish I could agree with her. Nothing will ever come close to the joy of skiing or boarding in fresh powder on a crystalline blue day.

Down the sandbar, Steve finishes setting up lunch from the coolers in the supply raft. Sandwiches, individual salads, and cookies are laid out on a folding table next to another cooler filled with beverages, including mini boxes of wine and cans of prosecco.

Not wanting to miss out on food, I hoist myself up and brush sand from my backside. I strip off my life vest and peel it open so it can dry in the sun while we eat. I'm soaked through except for a small area on my breasts and a patch on my back where the vest pressed against my skin.

The rest of the group appears as soggy and half-drowned as I do, with the exception of the bride and the guys.

Impressively, Twyla's managed to keep her tiara attached to her helmet through the class two and three rapids. Unlike me, she doesn't resemble a drowned cat. I'm guessing because I'm not vain enough to pull out a mirror and check on the state of horror.

Aiden dumps his vest on the sand, and stands in all his naked chest glory for a brief, shining moment. I was right about the muscles. He's all lean strength. The man has zero body fat. If we were stranded out here for weeks, I could use his abs as an actual washboard to clean our clothes. Sadly, he pulls on his T-shirt from the dry pack in the supply raft. Sad for me. Not him. It would be unwise for him to remain shirtless around a pack of horny women. Smart guy.

Hungry from the morning's adrenaline rush, I join the line for lunch. Food and a can of prosecco in hand, I find a spot next to Zoe in the half-formed circle. Funny how years after elementary school, we still gravitate to sitting in circles when gathered together.

Aiden drops down on the rocks to my left. He's only drinking water and I wonder if it's because he's working or in recovery. Would be rude to ask.

"How are you enjoying the day so far?" he asks the group, but I get the feeling he's really asking me.

Most of the women reply with answers about it being the biggest rush, a thrilling, exciting rollercoaster.

"Better than the best sex I've ever had," Twyla declares.

I nearly choke on my sandwich.

Aiden's shoulders shake with amusement.

"Have you heard that one before?" I whisper to him.

Keeping a smile on his face, he shakes his head no.

Zoe snorts. "You like sex that's cold, wet, and involves a lot of thrashing around?"

"Swallowing all those gross spurts and splashes of liquid? As if you're the kind who swallows, T," the redhead challenges my cousin.

Twyla shoots her a dirty look. "Cait!"

Realizing what she's said in mixed company, Cait hides her face in her hands, muttering, "I didn't say that in front of the guys. Ignore me."

"We were all thinking about sex and swallowing," Amy adds, clearly unwilling to contradict Twyla.

"No we weren't," Zoe mumbles. "Like that cake everyone calls better than sex. If that's true, you're not doing it right. Trust me."

"Preach, sister." I chuckle and stare at my feet as I stretch my hand toward her for a subtle high five.

"Oh, really?" Twyla asks, directing her question at me and Zoe. "You're having crazy, wild sex that leaves your heart racing and you completely out of breath to the point you feel like you're flying?"

Zoe smiles and nods.

"Bitch," I whisper.

She nudges me with her shoulder. "Yep. Be jealous."

"You too, Mae?" Twyla won't let it go.

Conscious of Aiden next to me, I know I can't lie. If I was having mind-blowing sex, I wouldn't be going to her wedding with Landon. Unless she's crazy and thinks I'm actually having sex with him and it's incredible.

"Not at the moment, no," I answer her. "Right now I'm eating the best sandwich of my life. I'm not sure if it's the near death experience we all recently survived or if it's simply that good. Where did you get these?"

Aiden tips his head toward me. "City Market."

"Wow. I had no idea. Good to know for all of my picnic needs." I finish my sandwich and follow up with drinking most of the can of prosecco. It's a small can.

The conversation moves on and returns to wedding planning.

Grateful I've avoided discussing my non-existent sex life, I stand and offer to help clean up.

Joining me, Aiden tries to takes my plate. "I'll do that."

"I can do it." I refuse to give it up. "Perfectly capable.

"I'm sure you are, but you're a client and that makes you a guest. Guests don't bus their own tables at La Belle Femme, do they?"

Unable to argue with his logic, I hand over my trash. "Thank you."

"No problem. I appreciate you wanting to help. You're one of the few people who have ever offered."

"Really?" I ask, surprised. When Twyla sitting surrounded by her bridesmaids catches my attention, my surprise fades. I imagine most clients would never think to lift a finger.

Steve collects trash and recycling into separate bags. Mitch hands out cookies, making him the most popular man on the trip.

"You see my point?" he asks, not pointing at my cousin, but it's clear from his head tilt he means her.

"People rarely see past their own immediate needs and pre-conceptions about roles." He sets his stack of plates on the table.

"You're a wise man, Aiden." *For a slacker and a possible addict*, I start to add in my head, but then stop myself. No qualifiers needed. I'm sure a lot of people would put me in the same category as him after I walked away from my career in LA to wait tables and snowboard. Now I'm wondering what rumors and gossip are going around about me. Maybe my mother is concerned about my slacker status and that's why she doesn't trust me to pick my own date for the wedding. Landon is a least a local celebrity even if he's notorious.

Standing near the boats, I dip my feet into the cold, clear water, and stare down at the small river rocks on the bottom. I'm the charity case in this date debacle. Inside I know this isn't true, but if that's how my mother and Mrs. Roberts are perceiving me, what does it matter?

Aiden comes to stay beside me. "You okay? Nervous about the rest of the trip?"

"I'm having deep thoughts about life and my mother." I laugh to cover up the truth.

"Being on the river is great for clarification." He gives me a slow smile. "Lots of time to think when not going through the bigger rapids."

"Will there be more giant, watery, death drops this afternoon?" I ask, only half kidding about the death part.

"Mostly some fun class twos with one nice three as the big finale. Nothing you won't be able to handle. For the final stretch, we run parallel to the road, so you've seen most of this part of the river."

"The river looks less intimidating from a car." I state the obvious

"Funny how proximity can change our perception, huh?" He bumps my shoulder. "You'll never look at the river the same way again."

The same could be said for Aiden. Landon is a kiddie pool compared to Aiden's wild, untamed rapids.

We're not in a place where I can ask him about his recovery. I want to respect his privacy because I'm all about healthy boundaries, but damn, I'm super curious. The only addicts I know are family and celebrities. Twyla's brother, Ailey, did a stint in a fancy place in Malibu and left early. He's still messed up. Jesse's brother died from doing stupid shit while drunk.

I'm not sure if I could ever take on being with an addict. I'm not that strong. And isn't there some rule about waiting a year after sobriety to start a relationship? Aiden will probably be long gone by that point. Getting together with him would be a huge mistake no matter if my body thinks otherwise.

Speaking of changing perception, my recent time with Landon hasn't magically transformed how I see him, not exactly. When we text, there've been glimpses of a better man in the cracks of his typical bravado. Sometimes I still see the teenage version I used to fool around with, who was cocky, but also funny and at times, sweet. Kind of like seeing a shadow out of my peripheral vision and thinking it's a person when it's really a pole or chair.

Could Landon be a secret romantic? I should ask Sage. He must still have some good qualities if she dated him. He could be the kind of man who needs to fall hard for the right woman before he's willing to change for the better. There's no way that woman is me, but I'm still not convinced he's irredeemable. He's not heartless monster.

"You never answered Twyla's question," Aiden says softly for only my ears.

"Neither did you." I cock my head to the side.

His cheeks round with his slow grin and he removes his sunglasses, revealing his warm brown irises. In spite of being nearly identical to Landon's color, Aiden's stare sends a buzz of electricity through body. My senses go on high alert.

I tell myself it's probably leftover adrenaline or anticipation of getting back in the kayak that's making my heart flutter. Or the fact he's asking about my sex life in a roundabout way.

"I love being on the river, the rush of the rapids, the slow, easy stretches where I can take the time to enjoy the scenery, the thrill of the build up, and the moment of satisfaction after completing a successful run." He lowers his voice further to a sexy, deep whisper. "All that being said, I'd never, ever say rafting is better than amazing sex."

My breath leaves my body in a whoosh as I sigh. Sweet heaven, his words. I have to look away or else I'll be forced to kiss him right this very minute. I'm only wearing a bikini, which is the same as underwear, so I'm basically naked and he's talking about amazing sex. I can't be expected to handle this.

I eye the river and think about throwing myself in the icy water to cool off.

"Your turn." He gently touches my wrist.

"I agree. No offense to your passion for your chosen profession." I don't elaborate because I'm not sure I've ever had sex as hot as the way he described rafting.

The skin around his eyes crinkles when he laughs. "You're not offending me. No one should ever go through life without experiencing mind-blowing sex."

Mentally, I fan myself. "Can't argue with that."

For the rest of the afternoon, I think about sex. Mostly sex with Aiden as I watch his strong arms paddle and his long legs tense inside of his kayak. His restrained power is one of the sexiest things I've seen.

There's something to be said for someone who commands their own power against nature. He isn't competing against another person to prove who's better or stronger. Instead, he faces off with nature and takes control. That's how I feel when I snowboard or ski, especially when I used to compete. Of course, I wanted to beat the other boarders' times and scores, but to do that I had to be the best at mastering the snow and conquering gravity. The high from adrenaline is a happy side effect of facing the power of nature and walking away unscathed.

We pass through beautiful canyons where pink hued cliffs climb high above us, calm water allowing us to float with the current to enjoy the scenery. I enjoy the smaller rapids, confidently navigating the rocks and whirlpools. When Aiden alerts us to a class three up ahead, I'm excited instead of petrified. Maybe because he goes behind me, loudly cheering as I twist and turn through the churning water.

By the time we finally reach the end of our ride, I'm ready to do it all again. I also might be a little horny and sexually frustrated.

Magically, our vans are parked along a gravel road near the river. I don't think I've ever been more excited to pull on leggings and a sweatshirt. Once all of the kayaks and the raft are loaded onto the trailers, we take turns changing clothes in the semi-privacy of the partially closed back doors of the vans. If someone, say Aiden, wanted a peek, all he'd have to do is walk by. This thought bothers me less than it probably should.

After everyone is changed, Mitch pulls another cooler from the back of a van and reveals more prosecco, wine, alcoholic seltzers, and sodas. "It's tradition we toast to a good trip."

No one is going to argue against this idea and we all happily grab a beverage.

Aiden shakes a can of soda, and then opens it, creating a spray of sticky liquid, which he aims at Mitch. "To another day on the river. We're the lucky ones."

We all clink our cans and boxes together.

"To Twyla." I raise my pink can high above her head. "May her married sex life be wilder than the wildest rapids!"

Sadly, she's probably already slept with Topher and knows what she's getting. I doubt they're waiting until marriage. Although, based on her earlier comment, she could be a born again virgin. She certainly isn't as innocent as she acts sometimes.

"Here, here," Zoe yells.

Others echo her with woots and "get it girl."

Twyla beams. "I'm getting married!"

In case anyone could forget for a minute.

Aiden meets my eyes. "This life is too short to be anything but spectacular."

I agree with him and hold my prosecco out to clink. Keeping eye contact, he taps his fresh can of soda against mine.

Why can't Landon be as cool as his brother? Why does Aiden have to be a river guide with questionable life choices? If I could combine the two of them, I'd make the perfect Roberts brother. The fact I'm even thinking Landon has good points to combine says a lot about his behavior the past few weeks.

We do same seats on the van ride to the hotel. Zoe falls asleep first; her head rests heavy on my shoulder. I try to stay awake to keep Aiden company while Twyla softly snores in the passenger seat, but my lids become too heavy to keep my eyes open.

"It's okay if you crash," Aiden tells me from the front. "Sun, adrenaline, and prosecco are the ultimate sleeping pill."

"Are you sure?" I ask with my eyes closed.

"I can take care of myself. Promise." I think he laughs at the end, but I'm already giving into the undertow of sleep.

TEN

AIDEN

UP SHIT'S CREEK without a paddle screwed.

I've spent all day thinking about Mae. From the moment I saw her at the fundraiser at the museum, she's been on my mind. I tried to resist flirting with her today, but have failed spectacularly.

Spectacular.

That's what she is.

Growing up, she was a cute kid, but the four year age difference prevented me from seeing her as anything more than a friend of my little brother's. Now that's changed in a day.

Honestly, my asshole brother doesn't deserve a shot with her, not even if it's for one date, one night. He's had years to come to his senses about her and has blown it by being driven only by his ego. I'm still stunned he manages to get any action at all given what a shit he is.

Twice today I wanted to advise Mae to dump my brother as her wedding date. Who cares what our mothers planned or if this is some lame ploy on my brother's part to get her into bed? Mae deserves better.

Someone like me.

Right.

The guy sleeping on my brother's couch.

That's going to change. And soon. The proceeds from selling my stake in the company I started, and walked away from, should hit my account within the month at the close of the third quarter. Combined with my existing assets, I'll be able to easily pay cash for a place around here and still have enough money to never have to work again if I don't want to.

Not too shabby for a guy who is currently guiding rafting trips.

I kept this information from Landon and my parents. The sale of the company won't be announced for another ten days. I asked for the delay to buy myself some time and distance. Luckily, my soon to be ex-partners agreed without too much protest. I'll keep stock options and they'll split the company two ways instead of three moving forward. Our goal was always to develop, grow, and then sell to a bigger fish in the market.

Walking two thousand plus miles through fourteen states has left me with a different perspective on myself and life. I don't need money or a big title to be happy. Amazing what doesn't interest me anymore. After focusing on checking off the boxes of success, now I can move on to actually living my life on my own terms. Well, almost.

When it comes to my growing feelings for Mae, I'm not being honest with anyone, including myself. Evidently, I'm still willing to put myself second to my brother out of a sense of obligation. No, it isn't that. Guilt. The two of us have always been competitive. The difference is I focus on the long game while Landon keeps track of every single point in each face-off.

Not sure if he considers me his competition anymore, given he thinks he has the upper hand at the moment. He only operates in a world with only winners and losers. Now he's focused on Mae. If he doesn't win her over, he loses. Not sure his pride could handle losing her to me. Instead of stopping this bullshit situation, I'm still doing my brother's bidding behind the scenes. The bigger thing to do in this situation is to allow him his shot.

At least I spent the day with Mae. With ten other people around and stuck in a kayak for most of it, but I got eight hours in her presence, watching the way her face lights up when she smiles or laughs, listening to her funny jokes, and guiding her to confront fears. No matter what happens after this wedding, I'll always have today.

Before returning the vans and equipment to our garage in Aspen, we need to drop the women off at the spa in Glenwood where they're spending the night.

If I had my way, I'd whisk Mae away from the group and bring her back with me. From her snarky responses and the few eye rolls I caught throughout the day, she isn't really into the whole bachelorette weekend. Can't blame her. I stuck close to her and Zoe most of the day because they seem the most sane and least grabby of the bunch.

Part of me feels bad for sticking Mitch and Steve with the wildest of the bunch. Mitch's heading to his first semester of college in a few weeks and is too young for these women. Steve's happily married and wears a thick gold band on his finger. That leaves me as the prime target. You'd think my shaggy appearance would deter the stares and casual touches. Yeah, right.

"We're here," I announce as I make the turn into the hotel's entrance. Not easy to navigate the hotel's driveway with a trailer, but I manage to find a strip of sidewalk where we can park both vans.

In the middle row, Mae and Zoe stretch and yawn, slowly waking up from their naps. The two women in the back never slept. Instead they've spent the short drive staring at their phone screens.

Next to me, Twyla grumbles about needing a real nap. "This tiara is giving me a headache."

"You can always stop wearing it." Mae's hand appears on

her shoulder. "We'll make sure everyone knows you're getting married. Even if we have to write 'bride' on your forehead with a Sharpie."

I press my lips together to keep myself from laughing.

"You're funny, Mae. I have a sash to wear, too," Twyla says, happily, unbuckling her seatbelt.

Meeting Mae's eye in the rearview mirror, we share a moment. She mouths "help me," and I reconsider my idea of driving away with her. If she pretends she's sick, it would be natural she'd want to go home and sleep in her own bed. Or mine.

If I had one.

There's not a chance in hell I'd bring her back to Landon's.

"Are you feeling okay?" I ask Mae, giving her an opening. "If you're sick, you can catch a ride back to Aspen with us."

Studying my face, she slowly nods her head. "I'm fine."

Because she didn't take my out, I resolve to not make a move until after the wedding and once I have my own place.

Sounds like a solid plan.

The guys are already pulling bags from the back of the van when I get out. For an overnight where most of their time will be spent in spa robes, there's an impressive amount of luggage. Mitch struggles with one bag that must be heavier than it looks.

"What do you have in here?" he asks when he sets it on the curb.

"It's probably stuffed with micro penis straws and inflatable pink dicks," Mae explains, loudly. A frazzled mother covers her son's ears as she passes us. Mae laughs. "Don't be offended, it's a bachelorette weekend. We're not kinky Russian hookers here for a sex convention. See my cousin's tiara? She's the bride."

Twyla hisses at her to be quiet while Zoe and I laugh.

"Russian hookers?" I ask, holding Mae's backpack for her. "Pretty specific."

Her eyes widen and she clamps both hands over her mouth.

"I'm so sorry. I didn't mean we were your hookers. I mean, I don't know why I would even say anything about kinky sex workers who may or may not be from Eastern Europe. Not my place to judge. No one told me anything. I swear. I'm going to stop talking now and go stand over there."

She follows her promise by walking away and straight into the hotel entrance without looking back.

Frowning, I wait for her to turn around to get her bag, the one I'm still holding. *Did she say my hookers?*

"What was that about?" I ask Zoe, who appears as confused as I am.

"No idea. I know she really hates penis straws. Had a mini rant about them before the bridal shower."

"Traumatic experience?" I'm even more lost, trying to make a connection between bachelorette accessories and prostitution.

Mae comes back, pushing a luggage cart. She gives me a shy, sheepish smile. "Ignore me. Sometimes I say inappropriate, random things."

"No problem." I don't ask for clarification because she seems embarrassed, and I don't want to add to that. Sometimes people get weird when they're coming down off of a big blast of adrenaline.

"I had a great day. It's so cool you're getting back to your roots after everything you've been through." She lunges for me and wraps her arms around me in a tight squeeze.

Shocked by her full body contact, I stumble back a step before catching my balance. Laughing, I glance over her head to see if anyone is paying attention to us. Thankfully, no one is standing around us, jaws on the ground. Safe from creating a scandal, I return her hug, instinctually pulling her closer. This feels right. She fits against me like she belongs here. With me. Reluctantly, I let her go.

When she releases her hold and steps away, I want to draw

her close again. "Thanks. I had a good day, too. It's good to see you again."

Can I say good more? Being this close to her erodes my vocabulary.

"Me too." She blinks up at me with her lips parted, her chest rapidly rising and falling.

I recognize her expression. She wants to be kissed. And I want to be the man who kisses her, more than she probably realizes. However, I'm not going to do it here in front of this audience. I made a pact with myself to wait and I don't break promises to myself.

Instead of leaning down and sucking on her full bottom lip like I want, I step away with a friendly squeeze to her shoulder.

"Good to see you again, Zoe." I nod at her friend.

"You too. You're officially my favorite Roberts brother. Expect to see me back on the river soon."

"Any time." I let my attention drift back to Mae.

Twyla steps forward and hugs me, discreetly handing me an envelope I assume holds a cash tip for us. "Thank you for making our day special. Consider yourself invited to the wedding. If you're in town in three weeks, I'm expecting you to attend."

"I'll be here."

After receiving hugs from both Mae and Twyla, the rest of the women come forward and create an awkward receiving line, hugging me and then Mitch and Steve. I try to bend forward to keep the body contact to a minimum. I'm mostly successful, only being squeezed by one or two of the bridesmaids.

Over the top of the final woman's head, I spot Mae grinning at me. She may not be saying I told you so aloud, but her eyes and smile clearly communicate the thought.

I'll suffer through hugging and groping at the hands of an exuberant bachelorette weekend if it means I can see Mae's beautiful face light up with amusement.

I'm so doomed.

Time's funny. Closing my eyes, I can easily imagine myself as Mitch—young, eager, and clueless. Hell, at thirty, I'm still mostly clueless. I guess the difference is now I know how much I don't know.

It's another ninety minutes before I walk through the door of the apartment. Inside, I find Landon and Easley sprawled on the couch, eating pizza, drinking beer, and playing some first person shooter video game.

Another reminder that despite our age, we're not that far away from being teenagers. Although I'm not sure my brother and his roommate will ever grow up.

"Hey, did you save any pizza for me?" I peel back the lid of the pizza box and find only crust.

"Didn't know if you'd be home," Landon mutters, not glancing away from the television.

"You could've had a hot date." Easley's gaze flicks over to the pizza box. "You can have the crust, if you want."

"Gee, thanks." Closing the box, I head for the kitchen. Not sure what I'll find to eat, but it has to be better than food that's been touched by their mouths.

"If you're looking for the chips and salsa, we ate those after the match earlier," Landon calls out.

"And the frozen burritos," Easley adds with a burp.

I open the fridge and stare at the shelves empty of edible food, wondering if I can make a meal from yellow mustard, a questionable jar of mayonnaise, beer, and three lonely slices of American cheese. Maybe if we had bread I could make a grilled cheese, but we don't. Resigned I'm going to have to go to the store, I reach for my keys on the hooks by the door.

"Want anything while I'm out?" I'm tired, hungry, and my

bedroom is occupied by the two of them. There's no point in thinking about crashing until they finish their game.

"Hey, are you going by the taco truck?" Easley asks, and then yells in triumph at the television. "Suck my dick, Landon. You're dead."

"How am I going to do that when I'm a corpse? You fucking freak." Landon throws an elbow at Easley.

I make a silent vow to bug my realtor about properties tomorrow. I need to move into my own place sooner than later.

Grumbling about living with cavemen, I take their order for tacos and head out.

When I get back, they're still sitting on the couch. I doubt they've moved in the time it took me to get food and drive home.

I drop a bag of tacos on the coffee table on top of the empty pizza box. Easley dumps out the contents and inhales two without pause. The man is a beast.

"You'll never guess who I had on today's trip?" I ask while pouring hot sauce on my first taco.

"Your mother," Easley responds without looking at me.

"No, idiot. Gwendolyn Roberts doesn't like to get wet." Landon steals a taco.

"Twyla London and her bachelorette party." I unwrap another taco. "Mae and her friend Zoe were there, too."

Landon inhales wrong and coughs on his food. "Mae told me they were going rafting. You were their guide?"

"I was."

He shoots me a quick dirty look while finishing his taco in two bites. "Coincidence, or did you request it?"

Inhaling, I try to ignore his jealousy. "We're limited on staff because it's the end of the season. Steve and I are the only two lead guys left besides the owners."

He continues shooting daggers at me.

I know he won't let it go, so I give him the answer he wants.

"For fuck's sake, no. I didn't request their trip."

"How was Twyla on the river?" he asks, finally giving me his attention. "I can't really imagine her paddling a kayak."

"In a tiara with a veil." I nod. "The official trip pics should be online by tomorrow morning." Part of the rafting package is access to purchase the GoPro pics and videos shot during the day.

"Are they all wearing bikinis?" Easley lifts his eyebrows. "Maybe there's a boob slip in some of the shots. Hello, nipple action."

Closing my eyes, I shake my head. "They're all wearing personal flotation devices, so there's zero possibility you're going to see any nipples."

"Fancy language for life vests, City Guy." Easley throws some shade at me with the city reference.

"Aren't tits basically personal flotation devices for chicks?" Landon asks. "Let's be honest though. Mae's aren't going to save her from drowning. Kind of small. Zoe's, too. Now Twyla has a rack that would save not only herself but another person from drowning."

A possessive growl rumbles in my chest. "When have you seen Mae naked?"

Landon laughs. "I was pretty familiar with her teen boobs, unless you forgot. Spent a lot of afternoons with them."

Right. "I meant recently."

"Who hasn't seen them naked? Those girls like to go skinny dipping in hotel Jacuzzis around town, especially on the full moon. It's pretty easy to find them if you know the right people." Easley stands up and burps loudly. "I gotta piss. Pause the game."

While I'm intrigued by the idea of Mae sneaking into hotel pools to go swimming naked, I'm bothered by Easley and Landon stalking them like wolves.

"Does everyone in town know about their habit?" I ask, annoyed.

"More than you'd think, but we don't want them to stop so we have to pretend we don't know," Landon explains without shame. "If they want to get naked in public, they can't expect privacy."

I'm not certain that's a valid excuse, but I'm too tired to argue morals with these two.

"Hey, speaking of Mae, thanks for helping with those texts to her last week. They totally worked. She went from barely responding to sexting."

My jaw drops open at Landon's words. "What are you talking about? She sexted you?"

He chuckles. "She isn't very good at it. No cleavage shot or anything good but she sent me a coded message that she wants to blow me."

Impossible.

"Show me." The tacos I ate sit like rocks in my stomach. "You're probably misinterpreting her words."

Still laughing, he pulls out his phone and throws it to me.

Scrolling through his messages, I find Mae's and open the thread. The final two messages are only emojis. "How are you getting a blow job from random food and a monkey? Are you the monkey?" This has to be a mistake.

"An eggplant is always a dick," he scoffs at me.

"You replied?" I cringe with regret for offering to help him. "With fruit?"

"Peaches are asses. How do you not know these things? Look closely. Totally a round, girl ass."

"For one thing, I don't spend my days figuring out how to make emojis sexual. Second, you sexted back about asses?"

"I told her I'm up for whatever sex she's interested in, even anal."

It's worse than I thought. Pressing the heels of my palms against my eye socket, I lean forward before scrubbing my hands down my face.

"Did she ask about me today? Or mention me? I never heard back from her after our last text," Landon asks, clueless as always.

"Strangely enough, your name never came up." I need to fix this. I tap reply window and begin typing.

"Hey, what are you texting?" He stands and makes a grab for his phone, but I'm quicker and block him, buying myself enough time to finish the message and send it.

"Fixing your mess. Can you try not to be a pervert between now and the wedding? You asked for my help and I'm trying. Work with me, okay?" I toss his phone in his general direction. "Be a gentleman for once in your life."

I want to tell him to grow up, but I'm the older brother living on his couch. As far as he knows I'm having an early mid-life crisis and not in any position to give him shit.

"What does this even mean?" He studies his phone. "Does the champagne mean blowing my load?"

"Jesus. No. It's a hint about the surprise you'll be sending her at the hotel. When she mentions it, don't act surprised."

"I'm sending her champagne? That shit's expensive. I hope you're paying for it because it was your idea."

"Yes, I've already ordered it on my card. You're welcome, by the way." Ungrateful little shit. "I'm going to go crash on your bed since you and Easley are playing video games."

"It isn't even eight o'clock, old man. We're going to go out tonight and you're going to bed." He tosses his phone down on the couch cushions.

"Wake me up before you head out and keep it down when you come home." I do sound like an old guy.

"*If* I come home. Big possibility I'll be sleeping elsewhere tonight." He bites his bottom lip and lifts his brows in case I missed the meaning.

"Yeah, good luck with that." I pick up my taco wrappers and the pizza box to dump in the kitchen trash.

"You need to get laid. If you can't manage it on your own, there's a discreet escort service in Aspen. Mostly Russian women." Landon smirks.

"Wait, Russian hookers?" His words trigger a memory and I walk back into the living area.

"They're not hookers. Escorts. Really hot model types. Not that I've ever paid for sex. Or had to."

"Did you mention anything to Mae about me and hookers?"

"Escorts, Aiden. Sheesh. Show some respect." He rolls his eyes and shakes his head like the little shit he is. "And the answer is no. Not that I can remember. Why? Is your secret out?"

I ignore the barb. "She said something about sex toys and prostitutes earlier. Didn't make sense."

"Was she communicating in emojis?" he says, sarcastically.

"Fuck off," I snark back.

"Just asking."

"You need to figure things out with Mae on your own," I tell him, my voice a low threat. "I can't be your puppet master."

Not waiting for his response, I stride down the hall to his bedroom. Exiting the hall bathroom, Easley bumps into me and apologizes for the stench. "Man, you better use the other bathroom. This one is off-limits for at least an hour."

"Got it. Going to crash in Landon's room."

Scrolling through my phone, I pull up the realtor's number and then send her a text asking about short term rentals available for immediate move-in, immediately like this week.

ELEVEN

AIDEN

I DON'T NEED or want a huge place. Two bedrooms so I can have an office. Near the mountain but I don't need ski-in, ski-out access. A view of nature instead of neighboring buildings would be nice.

This proves to be more difficult to find than I anticipated. Patricia's still optimistic she can find me a place before October, which is two weeks away.

When I approached my father about a friend needing a short-term condo rental, he didn't ask questions, merely sent me Patricia's contact information and told me she's the best agent in his office.

My mother is another story. Luckily, she's going to be distracted when the deal is announced next week. Focused on the whys and hows and the money involved will keep her occupied. Once the details are known, unfortunately, it will be the talk of the town, and the upcoming wedding—the social event of the season according to my mother.

I should probably get one of my suits out of storage in California when I go back for the final meeting. Before I left for Georgia to start my long walk up the East Coast, I thought about having a ceremonial bonfire of suits. When the time came to do it, I couldn't set fire to all of them, keeping back my two favorites, in case of future needs. I did burn all of my ties. I hate those silk nooses.

Today I'm looking at a two bedroom condo in the Viceroy in Snowmass. Not my first choice to live in a hotel, but Patricia's promised me it has a nice view of the ski mountain.

When I see the large deck facing the slopes, I agree right away.

"It comes fully furnished," she says, sweeping her arm out to the side like a car show model. "If you want. Of course you might have your own furnishing you want to bring in, and the owner can remove everything to storage for an additional fee."

"I sold everything except a few sentimental pieces, which are in storage in San Francisco. Furnished will be perfect." I eye the sofa. "On second thought, I'll buy a new mattress. If that's okay."

Her nose wrinkles before she smiles. "I would, too."

"Then we're all set. Draw up the lease agreement and I'll transfer the funds. Six months in advance, correct?"

"You'll be better off buying next spring if you can wait."

"I can. I'm learning to be a patient man."

Her smile is genuine. "I'm sure your parents are thrilled to have you moving home more permanently."

"My mother will be overjoyed when she finds out. Please keep this between us for now. I want to surprise them with the news."

Her professional expression of reserved interest falters for a second before she recovers. "Of course. Not a word from me."

Happy to have a place to live that isn't inhabited by semi-feral man boys, I want to share the news with someone.

One particular someone.

Mae.

Except I don't have her number.

However, I have a good idea of where I can find her.

I suddenly have a craving for crepes.

"Table for one?" The short blonde perks up, checking me out.

"I'm looking for Mae. Is she working tonight?"

"She's off today," she tells my pecs.

"Mae went to Rugby Fest. I think her boyfriend is one of the players." The tallest blonde gives me a dirty look.

The third blonde of the trio, asks, "Boyfriend? On the rugby team? Who?"

Curious to know the answer, I raise my brows and wait.

The tallest glares at her coworker. "You know. They're going to the wedding together."

"He isn't her boyfriend." I flash a smile. "Landon's my brother."

Odds aren't in his favor he'll ever be her boyfriend.

"Oh, you're the mountain man!" short and perky exclaims, clapping her hands like she just won the bonus round on a game show.

"Not sure about that. I'm Aiden." I give them all a brief wave. "Nice to meet you and thanks for the info. I'll head over to the park to catch up with Mae and watch my brother play."

Walking out of the restaurant and up the short flight of stairs, I'm self-conscious of them staring at me. A few weeks ago if I walked in there in a T-shirt and hiking pants, with my beard untrimmed and my hair long, they wouldn't have given me a second glance. Probably would've refused me service. Now that I've tidied up my hair and beard, I can feel the weight of their stares on my ass. It's a strange sensation to be ogled again.

They don't know anything about me, but they're each telling a different story inside of their head. I'd bet a grand nothing they come up with is close to the truth other than being related to Landon. Even that could be a lie.

I leave the car where it's parked and walk the few blocks to the field where the tournament is being held.

Amazing how a few superficial changes make a huge difference in how the world perceives me. While walking, I catch women noticing me. Some turn their heads as I pass, others whisper to their friends, a few point, being way less subtle than they imagine.

The only change I've made was to trim my beard and get a haircut. It's still longer than I used to wear it, but I'm too lazy to deal with it being short.

I'm grateful for my sunglasses blocking my eyes and creating a barrier between the gawking women and me. This way I can avoid eye contact. Wish I had brought my baseball cap with me instead of leaving it in the car.

The closer I get to the park, the more crowded the sidewalks get. Cheering carries through the streets even from blocks away. Based on what Landon told me, the Pitkin Rugby Club should be playing now or about to start their match against their biggest rivals, the Ambassadors from Denver.

Part of the charm of Rugby Fest is its small town feel. There aren't tickets or reserved seating. Dogs and kids roam around the edge of the park, sometimes crossing over onto the grassy pitch. Temporary white tents flank the north end of the park behind the black and red striped goal post. Children play in the little playground behind the beer garden.

I easily spot Landon and Easley in the middle of the field surrounded by the rest of their teammates. Behind them, risers are set up for spectators. Standing at the rope barricade, I scan the benches for Mae and Zoe.

"Hey, good looking, can I buy you a beer?" a woman shouts from inside of the beer tent.

Doubtful she means me, I ignore her and turn around to walk to the other side of the park. If I can't find Mae, I'll stick around to cheer for my brother and Easley. This afternoon is the final match and they've won every year for the past five. No pressure or anything.

Skirting the perimeter of the beer garden, I spot another set of risers on the other side of the Gosling's sponsored tent. I decide if I'm going to stick around for the match, I might as well have a Dark and Stormy, the signature Gosling's drink.

"Aiden!" I hear my name and spin around for the source.

Mae stands at the ropes, waving her arms.

I wave back, grinning at her like we haven't seen each other in months. So much for playing it cool.

"Finally," she yells, making her way through the crowded area. "I spotted you on the other side of the beer garden, but you didn't hear me when I tried to get your attention."

I show my ID to the bouncer guarding the entrance to the tents.

Mae greets me as soon as I'm waved through the gate.

I'm not sure if I should hug her or do the kiss on the cheek greeting or where we are on the scale between business handshake and an intimate embrace between old lovers. If it were up to me, I'd vote somewhere closer to the making out.

Because she has her hands full with drinks, we do an awkward, open half-hug where I go in for a kiss on her cheek but she isn't expecting it and I end up brushing my lips against the corner of her mouth before we both start laughing uncomfortably.

That went well.

"Here." She hands me a plastic cup. "I have an extra Dark and Stormy. It's yours if you want it."

I accept the cocktail. "An extra one?"

She nods and sips her straw. "The line is forever long and it's better to double up than spend the whole afternoon waiting for drinks or the bathrooms."

"Smart. Want me to get in line now to replenish your supply?" I offer, happy to repay the favor.

"No, come sit with us. We've taken over the front row by the goal post. Prime seating."

Drink in hand, she weaves her way through the crush of people lining the ropes. Sure enough, her group of friends occupies the first bench.

"Aiden!" Zoe greets me with a friendly smile. "Our favorite Roberts brother is here."

"Landon's not so terrible. Don't forget the champagne he had delivered. That was really sweet." Mae defends my brother, using my gift as the example. Exactly as intended. I'm glad they enjoyed it.

"True. And surprisingly it wasn't the cheap stuff. Maybe he is getting better." Zoe sounds doubtful.

The others all say hi and scoot down to make room for both Mae and I to sit. It's a snug fit, but I don't mind.

"What's the score?" I couldn't care less about who's winning or losing.

"Twenty-six us, nineteen for the Ambassadors."

"Good for them."

"You've already missed Easley splitting open his lip and punching a player on the other team." Clearly amused by this, Mae dishes the dirt on the game. "Then Landon tackled a guy during a time out. Words were exchanged, but sadly we don't have the scoop."

"We're thinking smack talk," Mara adds. "Maybe because Landon's been playing like shit."

Mae nudges her.

"Sorry. I know he's your brother, but he's kind of an ass," Mara apologizes, not sounding at all sorry.

"No worries about insulting me. I've been calling him LS

for Little Shit since we were kids. The abbreviation helped me get away with cursing in front of our mother. For years she thought I was saying Ellis. Hell, she probably still does."

"That's hysterical. Does he know and can we all call him that?" Sage asks from down the row.

"Go right ahead. I'm sure he's figured it out by now."

"I'm liking you more and more, Aiden." Sage extends her arm to tap her glass against mine.

"Me too," Mara adds, and Zoe echoes her.

"Me four," Mae says, with a small smile.

"Good." I lower my voice so only she can hear me. "I'd hate to be your second favorite Roberts brother." The crowd cheers when the Ambassadors score.

Studying me, her eyes widen with surprise. "You got your hair cut. That's why I almost didn't recognize you. Some lady in the beer garden thought you were a Hemsworth."

"Uh, I'll take that as a compliment. I think." I'm not sure why I feel uncomfortable with all this attention. I never had an issue with women in my former life.

"Trust me, it is. I like it." She surprises me by reaching up and dragging her hand through the shorter waves.

Her touch feels incredible and I want to ask her to keep going. Unable to read my mind, she drops her hand quickly and leans away. I'm going to have to work on my telepathy skills.

"Time to rejoin society I guess." I'm unsure about both the haircut and society.

"You make it sound like you're a hermit."

"In a way, I have been. Walking the Appalachian Trail solo meant basically being by myself for five months."

Her eyes widen with surprise. "After you were in rehab?"

Whoa. "Who told you I was in rehab?"

This has Landon written all over it. Not sure he'd outright lie and say I had a problem, but I can see him taking advantage of a misconception to his own benefit. Scraggly brother showing up after disappearing for almost half a year would provide him with good fodder for all types of stories.

TWELVE

MAE

EVERYONE APPEARS TO be watching the game. Maybe they didn't hear me. Everything will be fine.

Aiden takes a sip of his Dark and Stormy.

Oh, shit. I've shoved a drink at him. Way to fail at being supportive, Mae. "I'm sorry. I shouldn't have given you a drink. Don't feel peer pressured into drinking it. I'll take it back."

"It's fine. I swear to you, I don't have a drinking problem." He dips his chin and meets my eyes. "Promise."

I shoot him a look and drop my voice to a whisper. "Are you sure? I can get you a soda. I notice you didn't drink when we were on the river. It isn't a big deal."

"Swear. Did Landon tell you I went to rehab? Or did you hear that from someone else?" His voice is low and he sounds pissed off.

"No one told me. Not in those specific terms." I press my hand to the bare skin of his forearm. The soft hairs tickle my palm. I want to run my hand down his warm skin until I can slide my fingers between his and hold his hand to reassure him I'm not judging him. "I think it's admirable you realized you needed to make a change for the better."

"I did make a change. I'm still in the process of moving the pieces into place, but I'm getting closer to having the life I want. But—"

The crowd around us erupts in screams and jeering over something that happened in the game. I have no idea what's going on because I haven't been paying attention since I spotted Aiden strolling the perimeter of the park.

At first I was only checking out the hot guy in the tight gray T-shirt and faded jeans who strode through the crowd with a purpose. I hadn't been the only one to notice him. A woman I'd never met gripped my wrist to keep from swooning into a faint as she declared him the sexiest man alive. I'm only slightly exaggerating. Her friend is the one who asked if he was a Hemsworth. I had to do a double-take to confirm he wasn't and that's when I realized he was another infamous brother. I called out to him and offered him to buy a beer, but he didn't hear me or ignored a random woman offering him drinks. Smart of him.

Out on the grass, players are slowing peeling others off of the dog pile in the middle. I don't see Landon, but Easley's basically tossing guys from the top like he's peeling an artichoke.

"What's going on? Is this like finders keepers?" Sage scans the pile of men. "Lee's down there, too."

Zoe laughs. "How many matches have you been to over the last few years and you still don't know the terminology?"

"A lot." Sage stands on the bench to get a better view. "He's learned to live with it because he loves me. Along with a minor obsession with eighteenth century Scotland, this is one of my charming quirks. As I told Lee, I don't plan to figure out the intricacies of the sport. I've made a pledge and I plan to stick with it."

On my other side, Aiden stiffens. I'm not sure if it's what Sage said, a play on the field, or something else. Still feeling terrible for mentioning rehab, I don't want to make him uncomfortable by one of us saying the wrong thing again.

Zoe guffaws. "You're obsessed with *Outlander*. Don't try to make it sound like anything but your unhealthy fascination with naked Jamie Fraser."

"Who among us doesn't have that issue?" Mara asks.

We begin debating the merits of Sam Heughan. As an actor. Of course.

"Seriously?" Aiden exclaims.

I swivel my head to sneak a peek at him, expecting to see judgment in his face about us objectifying a man for his body. I'm about to tell him most women are here today because they enjoy the man candy. I open my mouth to speak, but clamp it shut as the crowd erupts into clapping and laughing.

Even Aiden is shaking with laughter.

"What's so funny?" I shoot him some side-eye.

"Landon got pantsed." He points at the field, clearly taking joy in his brother's situation.

I take his words as warning not to look, because I don't want to see Landon's naked ass in the broad daylight, or in moonlight. Not glowing in the dark or on an ark. Not on a bed, not even when I'm dead.

"Why are you staring at me?" Lifting his brows, he widens his eyes. "I'm still wearing my jeans."

"I don't want to see anything that can't be unseen." I cup my hand to the side of my head like a blinder on a horse to ward off any flash of temptation. "Tell me when it's safe to look."

Aiden's laughter gets louder. "The three of you all look like a row of the see no evil monkey emoji."

Closing my eyes, I turn my head and then reverse my hand, still protecting myself from any wayward peek. Only when I'm confident I won't have nightmares for life do I open my eyes. Sure enough, my friends have their hands over their eyes.

"Tell us when it's safe," Sage pleads. "I'm still not over the end of ski season flashing from a couple of years ago."

"Shrinkage is real," I whisper under my breath.

"You're safe," Aiden chuckles. "He pulled up his shorts immediately after he released the ball."

As if it's the World Cup final, a few guys around us grumble about not taking the match seriously enough. They're here for rugby and zero other fun. In this town, no one will be rivals for life over who wins or loses today. After this is over, everyone will probably end up at the same bars, trading insults and bonding over their awesomeness.

"You're not saying that to trick me, are you?" I still have my hand cupped against my face and I stare at him for confirmation.

"Why would I trick you into gazing upon the perfection of Landon's gluteus muscles? What good would that do me?" He ducks his chin and meets my eyes over the top of his sunglasses.

"Excellent point." I drop my hand. "For the record, you sounded just like him there. He definitely would refer to his ass as a gluteus of perfection."

"Like a peach?" Aiden asks, giving me a funny look.

Sage snorts loud enough for us to hear it. "Did Mae tell you she sent Landon a text meant for me? We like to communicate in hieroglyphics. It's our thing."

Mae's cheeks redden. "I think he deliberately misunderstood my meaning."

Smiling, Aiden shifts closer to me. "He can be a giant tool. If you haven't noticed."

"Totally." Nodding, I laugh along with him, although a small kernel of guilt forms in my chest. Landon promised he'd try to be less of a dickhead and he's mostly been successful. If Aiden weren't related, I don't think I'd have such mixed feelings.

We've been texting all week. After the river trip on Saturday, he texted saying he hoped we had a great time and ended it with all the flower emojis. No more lewd innuendos. Later, he sent a bottle of champagne to my room with a note about sharing with the rest of the girls. Totally unexpected and sweet.

The man in question makes the next score, earning bear hugs and high-fives from his teammates. Standing near our end of the field, he notices us cheering for him in the front row and flashes a huge grin.

"He isn't all bad." I give Landon two thumbs-up and add a loud, "Woot!"

He blows me a kiss. Two women a few rows behind me start screaming their love for him. Okay, so maybe the kiss wasn't for me specifically but all women in this general area. That would be something old Landon would do. Spread the love around.

"He has a few good points . . ." Aiden says, slowly and reluctantly, "I guess. I have to give him shit because he ruined my life by being born. Our feud began when he showed up. I remember being pissed when my parents brought him home and refused to take him back to the stork."

I laugh. "I think giving Landon a hard time is a favorite past time around here. He makes it so easy."

"I can call him off, if you want. You shouldn't have to suffer through a date with him," he says, sincerely.

Aiden's words confirm he's only looking at me as a friend. I can be that for him. Because it sounds like he needs the support. "That's sweet of you, but I'm fine. He's not been that bad. We've been texting and most of the time he's nice. Really nice. I'm beginning to think he's more awkward than an asshole."

Down the row, Sage snorts. "You're delusional."

Beside me, Aiden chuckles again. "We all deserve a second chance."

"I agree." I meet his eyes, hoping he can read the sincerity in my expression.

"Leopards can't change their spots," Mara states.

"Also a true fact," Aiden agrees.

"Amen to that." Sage stretches across Zoe and I to give him a high five.

He leans into me to slap her hand, his scent wrapping around me like a storm cloud of pheromones. This is what a man should smell like. Not cloying cologne or overpowering aftershave. Aiden's scent is crisp and fresh, like a summer rain or a morning after a night time snow. Inhaling greedily, I wish I could live in this bubble forever instead of in the real world full of complications and murky loyalties.

Once again, he returns to his own personal space, leaving me baffled and wanting more. He isn't the one to give me what I want. He has more issues than Landon, who at least wants to prove himself worthy, in his own messed up way.

A few minutes later, the game ends.

"We won!" Sage bounces up from her seat, jumping up and down. "We won!"

Around us, the crowd goes wild, jumping up and down, making the whole set of stands bounce. The super fans, who shushed us earlier, take off their shirts and wave them wildly over their heads, running onto the pitch to celebrate with the team.

Seconds later, Lee runs over and pulls Sage under the ropes, scooping her into his arms and kissing her like his life depends on keeping his mouth sealed against hers. Her feet dangle off of the ground as he carries her away.

"Did I miss the game?" Jesse jogs up to our group. He's wearing work clothes and has a fine layer of dust on his arms. A baseball cap hides most of his dark hair.

Mara squeals and stands to hug her boyfriend. "You're here!"

Jesse's dog, Fern, jumps on the bench and wags her tail.

"Aww, you brought my girl." I scratch her fluffy head, paying special attention to the spot she loves behind her ears. "Who's the best dog in the whole world? You are. Because you're smart and talented and fearless and beautiful."

"Hi to you, too, Mae." Jesse laughs at me, his dark eyes crinkling in the corners with amusement.

"Don't be jealous, Hayes." I kiss Fern's head and earn a lick to my cheek.

"You're Jesse Hayes?" Aiden asks.

"Aiden? How are you, man? I heard rumor you were back in town. Good to see you." Jesse extends his hand to Aiden.

They exchange a handshake followed by smacks to the shoulders in a loose, man hug.

Of course they know each other. We all grew up around here.

"You going to stick around and ski this winter?" Jesse asks him. "Cirque's open and the powder up there will blow your mind."

Mara giggles. "You sound like you're talking about Vegas circus acts and cocaine."

At her words, my eyes bug out and my mouth creates an awkward sound I try to pass off as a laugh. "Ha ha ha. No one is talking about drugs."

Aiden rests his hand on my shoulder, giving me a confused look. "You okay?"

"Sure. Of course. Oh, there's Landon! We should tell him congrats and pour a bucket of Gatorade over his head. Anyone bring a bucket? Or have a lot of Gatorade?"

Mara exchanges a look with Jesse before addressing me. "You sound weird."

"She's rambling like you do," Jesse tells her.

"That's it. Why are you babbling?" She focuses on me, her face scrunched up as she tries to figure out what's wrong with me. The woman is a talented veterinarian, but I don't think she can diagnose embarrassment.

Landon comes to my rescue, plowing through the ropes and picking me up, his sweaty body odor swarming my senses while I can feel my skin sticking to his damp shirt.

Everything happens so fast. One minute I'm on the ground and living my life. The next Landon's tongue is in my mouth.

THIRTEEN

LANDON

SHE'S LAUGHING AND squirming against me as I lay one on her.

"Put me down, Landon. You're all sweaty and gross." She swats at my shoulders.

Obliging her, I set her on her feet and then drape an arm over her shoulder.

"Ugh, being trapped in the hell portal of your armpit isn't better." Mae shoves me away and puts some distance between us. "You need a shower."

"Sage didn't seem to mind Lee's stench. He's a sweatier bastard than I am." I'm too happy to give a shit about the South African giant currently making out with Sage.

Easley tackles me from behind. "We won. Motherfucking champions!"

"We're going to need to turn a fire hose on these guys. They're out of control," Mae mumbles under her breath.

I hope she means for my brother. Because hell yes I saw him all cozied up to her during the match.

Fuck that.

During time-outs or even running toward their goal, my

attention kept wandering over to the two of them sitting together. Laughing and touching her like he was trying to get in her pants.

We have a pact. He's supposed to help me have a shot with her.

Not fucking flirt with her.

Even from yards away it was easy to spot him making his move on Mae.

He's sitting on the sidelines while I'm kicking ass and fucking shit up to win this tournament.

If anyone is getting Mae's attention today, it damn well better be me.

So I picked her up and kissed her.

Fuck yeah I did.

Staked my claim in front of Aiden and all of her friends.

Playing nice on text messages wasn't getting me anywhere. He can sit there with his words and his haircut, but I was the one with my tongue in her mouth.

Action always wins over discussing feelings and shit.

I grin at Mae. "Thanks for the victory kiss."

"Uh, I don't think I had much choice." She laughs it off.

"We're going back to the club to shower and change. Everyone meeting at Little Annie's for the celebration?" I ask the group, but my attention is solely on Mae.

Her cheeks are flushed from our kiss and her eyes are a little dazed. I think I kissed her stupid. She wouldn't be the first woman I've left speechless.

Hugging Mae again, I shoot my brother a dirty look over her shoulder. "Aiden, you can join us if you don't have anything better to do."

"Thanks." He nods, returning my glare with one of his own. "Maybe I'll tag along to the club . . . since I have nothing better to do."

"Let's go," Lee says. "We're lining up for the presentation

of the cup."

"Champions!" Easley attempts to pick him up.

"Lift me off the ground and you're going to pay," Lee snarls at him. "Ask yourself how attached to your balls you are. Do you want to keep them?"

"Champions!" Easley jogs toward the rest of our teammates.

"He's a very excited gorilla today." Sage grins. "Anyone else think he'll shave #1 in his chest hair like he did two years ago?"

Zoe makes a small gagging noise in her throat. "I need to go. Justin's competing in the rodeo tonight in Glenwood. I think I'm going to surprise him."

"I'll join you," Mae declares.

"We have to go home and feed the cats," Mara tells Jesse. "You know how they get destructive if their dinner is late. I don't want George locking Tapper in the bathroom again in another hostage situation."

Boy, I dodged a crazy cat lady nightmare with her.

"Come on, Mae. We need to celebrate tonight. It won't be the same without you." I give her my wide-eyed innocent look.

"I'll see." She points behind me where the entire team is lined up and ready. "You need to accept your trophy."

"Stay here. I'll be right back." Jogging backward, I keep my eyes on her, and more importantly on Aiden.

I don't trust his supposedly selfless motivations anymore.

I might be a winner today, but I suspect he's playing a long game.

Per usual, Aiden's the third wheel.

Grumpy despite our championship, I gather my shit together and stomp over to them.

"You ready?" I ask, not caring if my tone is curt.

"Let's go, LS." He stands and stretches his shoulder with his arm across his chest.

Sage giggles. Great. He probably told her how funny he was as a kid coming up with my nickname.

"Aren't we a little too old for you to still be calling me that stupid name?"

"When you grow out of being a little shit, I won't have a reason to use it anymore." He smirks.

If we weren't surrounded by a crowd of fans, including kids, I'd deck him right now. My fist opens and closes with the satisfying thought of throwing a punch at his stupid face.

"Do it," he goads me. "I can see you want to hit me. You have an obvious tell. Don't wait for permission. Just go for it."

"Fuck off," I growl at him, taking a step closer.

"Whoa. You need to cool off." Lee squeezes himself between us. "What's the deal? We just played an incredible match and you two want to fight?"

I don't want to say too much in front of Sage because I know she'll run and tell Mae. "Nah, we're fine."

"Sure," Aiden confirms. "Great. I think I'm going to skip the party tonight. I'll see you back at the apartment."

After he says goodbye to Sage and Lee, he gives me a one fingered salute. "Landon."

I glare at his back as he walks away.

"I don't even want to know what that was about." Sage shakes her head. "None of my business. Not my circus and definitely not my monkeys."

Lee slings his arm around her shoulders. "I think I'll shower at home before we join the party. We'll catch up with you later."

Fucking Aiden. I blame him for pissing on my celebration. The man is a killjoy. Well, I'm not going to let him fucking ruin my night.

Dark hair spills over my chest, resembling Mae's. The woman

wrapped around me is naked and my hand rests on one of her ass cheeks. Mentally, I give myself a high five.

The events of last night are hazy and choppy. I remember going to Little Annie's and challenging everyone to do a shot for every point we scored. Given the final score of the match was fifty-six to twenty-nine, no one took me seriously enough to try to win that challenge. However, I drank a shit ton of whiskey and beer. I wish I could recall Mae showing up at the bar and how I charmed her into bed. I need to remember for next time.

For now it's enough to know I'm the one she came home with and had sex with. I'm not one hundred percent sure we fucked, but the odds are in my favor. My morning wood thickens at the thought of another round before I head home.

When I gently tug on a long strand of wavy hair, the owner murmurs, "Good morning," in a husky voice that is most definitely not Mae's.

Disappointed, I make the best of the situation by having morning sex with my new friend before saying goodbye and getting the fuck out of her hotel room.

~~~

Shoving open the door with my shoulder, I find Aiden sitting on the couch, talking on the phone.

Spotting me, he holds up his index finger, silently telling me to keep quiet.

I don't say anything, but I loudly drop my stuff on the floor. Stepping into the kitchen, I open and close a bunch of cabinets and then turn on the sink.

The jerk shoots me a dirty look as he goes out to the balcony to continue his super important call.

I see he's made coffee, so I pour as much as I can fit into a jumbo travel mug and dump the rest down the drain. Petty as fuck, but I don't care.

He doesn't seem to be wrapping up his conversation any time soon, so I decide to take a shower. When I come out of the bathroom, steam fogging up the mirror, I find him in the kitchen making another pot of coffee.

"Did you tell her I went to rehab to make yourself look better? Low, even for you. You don't know shit about my life because you never ask, only assume the worst."

I shrug off his accusation. "I didn't tell her anything more than you were sleeping on my couch. Guess she came to her own conclusions."

"You don't need to worry about that anymore. I'm moving out," he tells me, not bothering to make eye contact. "And I'm flying to San Francisco tomorrow for meetings all week. I'll be moving my stuff over to Mom and Dad's house this afternoon."

"Wait, no. I'm throwing you out. You don't get to steal my thunder, asshole. I want you gone." I block him from leaving the narrow kitchen.

"Are you going to punch me? You're balling up your fists. What's pissed you off so much?" His calm voice pisses me off more.

"You think you're so slick telling me you'll help me out with Mae, give me advice, yet the whole time you've been putting moves on her for yourself. It's obvious you like her. I saw the two of you together yesterday. It made me fucking sick." I spit out the last words and step back.

"Give me a break, Landon. You didn't see shit yesterday while you were in the middle of playing. Fuck off with your bullshit." He shoves past me and strides back into the living room.

I notice he doesn't deny liking her. "You know what? She isn't interested in some loser who fucked up his life and had to crash on his younger brother's couch. You don't have a chance. Never did. Not when we were in high school, not now."

He laughs, and it comes out like another way of telling

me to go fuck myself. "Right. You made your point yesterday by grabbing Mae and kissing her in front of everyone. Did you notice if she kissed you back? Didn't look that way from where I stood."

Lunging at him, I try to take him down like I did when we were kids. Bastard ducks out of the way and puts me in a headlock.

"Don't." His voice is a low, menacing rumble in his chest I can feel where my head makes contact. "I'm going to count to ten and then you're going to stop acting like you're having 'roid rage. One, two . . ."

For every number he says out loud, I silently echo it with a fuck you.

"Ten. Ready to act like a man instead of a toddler?" He tightens his grip for a second before releasing me and then quickly stepping away.

Rubbing my neck, I glare at him. "When did you say you were leaving?"

"As soon as I pack up my stuff."

"Good."

"Landon, it doesn't have to be like this. If you seriously think you have a legitimate shot with Mae, take it. If she genuinely likes you, I'll step out of the ring. But it's going to be her decision." He speaks calmly and deliberately, maintaining eye contact with me.

I don't know if he's insulting me or what. Not to be the first to back down, I stare at him and cross my arms.

"I'll be gone all week. Here's your chance to win her over before the wedding. I wish you luck."

He walks toward me and I brace myself in case he decides to throw a sneaky punch. To my surprise, he cups my shoulder and gives me a sad smile.

"We're always going to be brothers. Can't change blood."

I don't say anything back, just nod and head into my room, giving both of us some space.

After he leaves, I text Mae and ask her to meet me for a drink this week.

FOURTEEN

AIDEN

NEVER DID I imagine I'd end up in a strange love triangle involving my brother, if that is what's going on here. He's never been my rival, even if he sees me as his. This was supposed to be a straight line from point A to point B with me being the arrow showing the right direction. I should've known better. Cyrano doesn't get the girl at the end.

Of course when I offered to help him, I didn't know the full story. I agreed because he asked. Developing feelings for Mae is on me and I own that. I had no reason to think I'd fall for her. Zero expectations she could ever possibly feel the same way about me. Nor did I realize what a hot mess Landon was when it came to women, respecting them, and knowing how to treat them right. Not only is he a disaster, he's cocky enough to not want to change. His ego's big enough to tell him he's always right, and if we don't like it, we can go fuck off. I believe that last part is an exact quote from one of our recent text conversations.

While I've been out here, I guess he's been trying to get Mae to go out with him and she's blown him off. I don't even feel slightly bad he's crashing and burning. Nor am I surprised.

To satisfy my curiosity, I asked for details. It's the train wreck I imagined. Proving he's learned nothing from how I interacted with her or the thoughtful gift, he's resorted to the emoji game. Unsuccessfully. At least he hasn't sent her a dick pic. Unable to stop myself, I tell him to cool the sex emojis and just tell her how much he's looking forward to being her wedding date next weekend. There's a slim chance he doesn't ruin this simple instruction.

Definitely a good thing I moved out and put some distance between us. Mom was thrilled when I called her last Sunday morning to ask if her offer of the guest room was still open. No questions asked and she put fresh linens on the bed for me. Landon avoided their weekly dinner together, claiming exhaustion from the match. I knew he was lying and he'd know I knew, but I let him do what he needed to do. Having dinner with her and Dad alone meant I could give them the full story on the sale of company and what that meant for me.

Mom cried, relieved I hadn't become a scofflaw or vagrant.

Dad's eyes watered with pride and he kept patting my shoulder, telling me good job.

She went full waterworks when I shared I'd signed a six month lease with a clause forbidding sublets. With a promise to be back, I left them and Snowmass behind for the last corporate meetings of my life. Hopefully.

Now I'm sitting at the Denver airport mid-day on Monday, a week after I left, waiting for my connecting flight into Aspen, carrying a garment bag containing two designer suits and my small carry-on.

To occupy myself before boarding, I scroll through the Aspen Coalition social media, seeing bits of Mae's personality in every post and picture. In the ones about the fundraiser, I spot myself in the background of two. Before my haircut and beard shearing, I really did resemble a mountain hermit. I hadn't realized how much I'd changed until I saw photographic evidence.

I'm still not ready to forgive Landon for whatever seeds he

planted in Mae's head about me or misconceptions he perpet-
uated. Nor am I blaming her for any crazy theories she formed
based on Landon's misinformation campaign and my own
reticence to talk about details of my life.

The butterfly doesn't give a play-by-play while transforming
inside of the cocoon.

Mae is worth fighting for. The kindling of the connection
I felt for her when I first saw her at the museum has sparked
a wildfire inside of me. I can't walk away. Not now. Maybe
not ever.

"This seat taken?" a woman asks, standing next to me.

"No." Without glancing at her face, I move the garment
bag and then hang it on the handle of my suitcase. "All yours."

"Aiden? I thought that was you."

Finally, looking up I recognize Sage. "Hey. What are you
doing here?"

"Waiting for a plane. What else?" She laughs and I join her.

"Heading home?" I ask, because I'm full of stupid questions
today.

She sits down and bends her knee. "I am. Had a quick trip to
Chicago to see my family. I have a niece who turned one while
we were in South Africa. I owed her a giant, stuffed unicorn
and as much buttercream as she could handle before barfing."

"Did you accomplish your goals?" I shift to face her.

"Most definitely." She peers around me. "Checking out the
Coalition's social media?"

I forgot my phone was on their Instagram account. "I made
a donation at the fundraiser, but I don't really know much about
their work. Doing some research."

"You probably already know this, but Mae runs their social
content." Her look tells me we both know I do. She doesn't
harp on catching me; instead, she asks, "What's in the fancy
garment bag?"

"Suits."

She glances at the bag again before meeting my eyes. "You don't seem the type."

"Definitely not. Never really was, but in my former life I needed them for important meetings with very important people." I grimace. "Always hated them."

"Understandable. I'm not the office and suit type myself. That's what's so wonderful about living where we do. Less pressure to conform." She tucks a strand of her pale blond hair behind her ear. In her colorful long skirt and tank, she's the exact opposite of a dull, corporate drone.

"You get it."

"You'll find a lot of us are kindred spirits."

"Good to know. A lot has changed since I've been away. I get the feeling I need a new group of friends." Without saying too much, I hope she hears the meaning behind my declaration.

Boarding is called for our flight and we join the line.

"Speaking of, Mae's picking me up at the airport. If you need a ride back to your place, I'm sure she'd be happy to drop you off."

"Thanks, but I'm not really on your way." I want to slap my own hand over my mouth for refusing. It's been more than a week since I've seen or spoken to Mae and now I'm passing up an opportunity.

"No problem. Let me just send a text and it'll all work out." She taps on her screen for a moment and then smiles at me. "All set."

The short flight is uneventful. Once we land, Sage waits for me on the tarmac.

"Did Mae agree?" I ask as we walk into the tiny main terminal.

"Of course she did." Sage's smile is sly.

We quickly pass through baggage and out to the arrivals pick-up area where we are promptly greeted by both Lee and

Mae. She looks amazing in a pink, flowy dress, her dark hair swept off of her face in a bun at the crown of her head. I can't help the grin that spreads over my face when I see her.

"Surprise!" Lee says, sweeping Sage into his arms and giving her a passionate welcome home kiss.

Mae gives me a small wave and I decide to go in for a cheek kiss. Stepping forward at the same time she does, we get our feet tangled and I drop my garment bag as we laugh, trying to figure out if we're hugging or not. With my hand on her shoulder to still her, I duck my head to kiss her cheek at the same moment she turns to give me the other one. Our lips accidentally brush together. I both feel and hear her intake of breath, but neither of us pulls away. Encouraged, I press my lips to hers in a real kiss, our first.

Her fingers grip and flex on my bicep and she returns the pressure for a second before her lips curve into a smile. I give her another soft peck, wondering if she feels the same hum of energy spreading through her body like I do. Unplanned and awkward, it's still my favorite first kiss.

Grinning up at me, she whispers, "Hi. What are you doing here?"

"Coming home." I run my hand down hers until our fingertips touch.

Sage giggles, and I'm not sure if it's at me or she's giddy to be with her boyfriend. "I ran into Aiden in Denver and told him you could give him a ride home. That was before I knew Lee was going to surprise me."

"Honey, you texted me from Denver and—"

Sage cuts him off with another kiss. "And I'm so excited you decided to come meet me. I've missed you. And the dogs. I'm dying to go home. Mae, do you mind still giving Aiden a lift?"

Before either of us can confirm or protest, she's leading Lee by the hand toward the parking area. "Mae, call me later this week and we can discuss what we're wearing to the wedding. Bye, Aiden!"

An awkward silence settles around us after her departure.

"We were set up, weren't we?" I finally ask.

"Totally. She messaged me this morning from Chicago and that's the last I heard from her. I had no idea you were flying in today, too."

"Interesting. While we were waiting in Denver, she texted someone and I assumed it was you."

"Nope." She laughs, and it's becoming one of my favorite sounds.

"You don't have to bring me home. I can catch a cab or Lyft. No big deal." I want to see her, but not because she feels obligated.

"I don't mind driving you down valley. I could use a trip to the big Whole Foods." She spins her keys around her finger.

We shared our first kiss a few minutes ago and she's thinking about grocery shopping? I know it was unplanned and a little less than smooth, but come on. I can do better.

I step into her space and catch her keys in her hand. "Can you hold that thought for a second?"

She nods, her brows scrunched together in confusion.

"Good."

I kiss her again, this time on purpose. And she kisses me back, pressing into my body, encouraging me. Wrapping my arms around her, I hold her close as I continue to kiss and explore her mouth. Her tongue sweeps against mine, hesitant at first before I moan at the contact.

My ability to be rational and tell myself this is a bad idea fades with each passing second. What began as an accident has turned into a curbside make out.

"Wow," she whispers. "That was . . ."

"Unexpected?" I suggest, my voice lower and more gravely than normal.

"Amazing is what I was going to say, but unexpected works, too." She touches a fingertip to her full bottom lip.

Unable to resist, I kiss her again.

A car honks twice as it passes us. Peeking through one eye, I see Lee and Sage wave as they drive out of the lot. It's enough to remind me we're not alone and have zero privacy standing outside of the terminal.

Mae laughs against my mouth. "I have wonderful friends."

I press a soft kiss to the corner of her lips, but don't loosen my hold on her waist. "The best."

"Want to get out of here? I can still drive you down valley." She tips her head back to meet my eyes, so I kiss the tip of her nose.

"You could, but I don't live in Basalt any more." Releasing her, I pick up my garment bag, which is laying on the ground.

"Did Landon kick you out?" she asks, frowning as she steps off of the curb.

"Not exactly. I think we came to the same conclusion almost simultaneously. I'm back in Snowmass. At least temporarily." I hesitate to tell her more. Unlike our spontaneous kiss, I want to make sure I get this next part right. And that means taking things slow, at least until this stupid wedding is behind us.

"At your parents' house? How's Gwendolyn?"

"My mother is fine. Thankfully, my stay in the Roberts' guest suite was only for a few days. I have something up at the Viceroy." I'm not lying, just omitting the full details of the truth, which seems to be my deal lately, at least when it comes to Mae.

"Wait, when did you leave Landon's place? He's been texting me all week, but never mentioned you were gone." She stops next to an old, yellow bug that predates both of us. "Keys, please."

I toss the set to her and step beside the passenger door. "I left a week ago to attend meetings in Palo Alto and moved my things in the Sunday before."

"After Rugby Fest?" She ducks down to sit and then unlocks my door.

The heavy door creaks when I open it. "How old is this thing?"

"Ancient, just the way I like it. Don't comment about the rust." Laughing, she turns the key and the engine sputters to life. "To the Viceroy, then?"

I nod. "If you don't mind. Do you have plans? I could buy you dinner as a thank you for the ride. Pizza okay?"

Taking her eyes off the road, she frowns. "I have to go into work. I'm usually off on Mondays, but with Topher and Twyla festivities this weekend, I've switched up my schedule and am working every night until Friday. In fact, this whole week is being sucked up by wedding stuff, and I'm not even getting married or in the wedding party. It's insane and I can't wait for the whole thing to be over. Rain check?"

"Definite rain check. What are you doing Sunday morning?" I ask as she drives us up the winding road toward Snowmass.

"You'd think having to attend the rehearsal dinner on Friday and the wedding on Saturday would be enough time to properly celebrate their love, but you'd be wrong. There's a brunch and official send off Sunday morning at the Mountain Club. Rumor has it the happy couple will be departing in a hot air balloon like they're leaving Oz."

I chuckle at how riled up she is about this wedding.

Because she has to get back to Aspen for her shift, she drops me off with a quick goodbye. I give her a peck on the cheek, not wanting to start anything more before we have a chance to talk.

Only as I watch her little yellow car disappear down the mountain do I realize I still don't have her phone number. Not going to ask Landon for it, and trying to get it from my mother is an even worse option.

Scoring an invitation to the rehearsal dinner will be easier and require selling less of my soul.

FIFTEEN

MAE

THIS ONE WAS different. Accident or not, it turned deliberate, like he had something to prove and could only do it with his tongue in my mouth.

There's an expression about comparison being the thief of joy and it's never more true than when applied to the Roberts brothers and their kissing abilities. Let's just say that if I knew in high school what I know now, I would never have wasted so many hours letting Landon play hockey with my tonsils using his tongue as the stick. Sadly, from what I experienced at Rugby Fest, he hasn't improved. If ten years of kissing every woman who will let him can't up his skill level, what can?

No one has enough time or patience to teach him. Certainly not me.

For the past week he's been texting and bugging me about getting together before the wedding to "pregame" our date. And I've blown him off every single time. The man's persistent, but also stubborn.

I'm trying to give him every benefit of a doubt I possibly can, but he seems to ruin each chance at redemption. For example, when I thanked him for the champagne he sent to the spa, he grumbled about overspending and what difference does it make if he bought the cheap stuff. Weird, like he was mad about making a nice gesture when no one forced him to do it.

I don't understand him. Sometimes he's sweet when he's not texting me man candy emojis.

Every time I bring up one of his sweet gestures or thank him for a compliment, he backslides into acting like a jerky teenager.

Then there's Aiden with his advanced level kissing prowess and all of his ugly baggage. When I ran into him at the airport, which forever will be known as the site of *the kiss*, he mentioned meetings and was carrying a garment bag. I wonder if he had a court hearing or trial. Hopefully, all of the bad stuff is behind him now.

Right before *the kiss,* he mentioned coming home. If it's true he's here to stay, we'll have plenty of time to sort rumor from fact post wedding.

Ah, the wedding. Topher and Twyla better live happily ever after 'til death do they part.

As if sensing my thoughts drifting toward this coming weekend, my phone rings with a call from my mother.

I've been avoiding her this week, too. Her worry over my choice of clothing is bordering on obsession. Probably shouldn't have joked about showing up naked as that might be what sent her over the cliff.

Against my better judgment, I accept the call.

"Mae? It's Mom. I'm calling to confirm you have something for both tonight and the wedding tomorrow. Oh, and the brunch. Don't forget Sunday." She speaks in a fast stream, not allowing a breath or pause for interruption.

I remain quiet as I stand in my bedroom, facing my closet. Her timing is eerily perfect.

"Are you there? Hello? Did I get your voicemail?" Mom's irritation increases with each new question.

"I'm here. I wasn't sure if you wanted me to speak or only listen." Switching to speaker, I rest my phone on the shelf of my closet.

"What are you wearing?" she asks, ignoring my snark.

"Right now? Leggings and a T-shirt I pulled out of the laundry. I'm not sure if it's even mine." I'm lying because I'm dressed for work in black jeans and a black ruffled blouse.

"Margaret, this is why I worry. Do you need me to meet you tomorrow to go shopping? I don't know why you didn't ask for help sooner. If we can't find anything in the shops, it's too late to drive to Denver and be back for the dinner." Her sigh is loud and full of disappointment.

"I have suitable clothes. Why are you so worked up about this weekend? Is there a secret betting pool on who's going to create the next family scandal?" I touch the hem of the green dress I bought for the ceremony and reception. It isn't the Prada silk I ogled in the window, but a good knock-off I could actually afford.

For tomorrow night I have a tailored black jumpsuit with ruffles on the neckline. Elegant and simple, it won't call attention to me, and if I need to make a quick escape, the black will hide me in the shadows. I'm sure having to be topless while peeing would horrify my mother, so I don't go into details about my choice.

Lost in my thoughts, I don't realize my mother never replied to my joke about family scandal.

"Mom? Is there a betting pool?" I ask, stomach sinking at the thought I'm probably in the lead.

"No, of course not. You know we're not into gambling . . . we don't even buy lottery tickets." Now she's not chatty? Something's up.

"But?" There's clearly more she's not saying. "Worried about someone creating a scandal?"

"Not to gossip, but Twyla told your aunt that she and Topher had an argument earlier this week," she whispers the last part.

"Are they calling off the years of matrimonial bliss because they had a disagreement? They're probably overwhelmed and stressed. I know I am, and I'm not the one getting married."

"Of course they're not calling things off. Don't be silly."

"Who are you trying to convince? Me, or yourself, Mom?" I chuckle. "Better to not get married than go through a divorce. Less paperwork."

"Margaret, this isn't funny." Full name and mom voice means I'm in trouble. "Twyla was very upset. Evidently, they never argue."

This news doesn't surprise me. I can't imagine Topher working up the passion for a big fight.

"What did they fight about?" I make my voice serious. "Is Twyla refusing to change her name? I know I would. Twyla Tierney is a mess."

"Please be mature about this. You should call your cousin and see how she's doing. I'm certain she'd love to hear from you."

"No, she wouldn't. All of her college friends are arriving from out of town. She'll have plenty of girlfriends to lend a supportive ear. I'd only say something inappropriate."

She sighs again. "You're right. Okay, I'll let you go. Send me pictures of your dresses."

"Of course." I'm already planning to accidentally forget.

When we disconnect, I sigh, echoing my mother. *Three more days.*

A new text from Landon pops up on my home screen.

Can't wait for tomorrow night.

Thinking if I respond, he'll calm down, I send a thumbs-up, and then drop my phone into my bag.

Sage and Lee pick me up outside of my apartment to drive to the hotel, and I'm happy to have their company. I'll be meeting my "date" in the bar because this isn't prom and we won't be leaving together.

At this point, I feel like I'm the uptight cop in a buddy movie who ends up handcuffed to a crazy criminal. Opposites don't always attract. So far it's a pretty lame comedy bordering on a tragedy. Based on my experiences over the past six weeks, there's a thin line between laughter and crying.

Two valets greet us when we arrive at the hotel, opening our doors as soon as Lee puts his Land Rover into park.

Discreet signage directs us to the pool deck for the cocktail hour. We swing through the bar in the lobby to find Landon. He's sitting at the bar, chatting up the bartender—a beautiful woman with curly black hair and olive skin.

"Ahem," I clear my throat a few feet behind him.

He spins his stool to face us. "Ah, here's my beautiful date for the evening."

From his glassy eyes and sloppy smile, and the lovely beer breath, I'm guessing he's done some pregame drinking.

Delightful.

"Ready?" I don't bother with niceties. After he grabbed me and kissed me at Rugby Fest, I'm keeping my boundaries firmly in place around him.

"To party? Hell yeah." He steps off the stool and catches his foot on the lowest rail. Hopping on one foot, he untangles himself. "Let's go."

Lee's wearing a well-tailored black suit, gray shirt, and a gray tie accented with a silvery blue. Landon's in a light blue dress shirt and blue dress pants. No jacket. I wonder if he knows he needs to wear a suit for tomorrow. If I cared, I'd remind him.

We catch an elevator to the pool level and step off into an elegant foyer, decorated with aspen branches and roses.

"And so it begins," Sage says close to my ear. "It's a blessing my own mother isn't here to take notes for my wedding."

Pinching her elbow, I pull her to a stop and whisper excitedly, "Did Lee propose?"

"Not yet, but my dad made a weird comment the other day that makes me think Lee called him to ask for my hand." Love shines bright in her eyes.

"He's a traditionalist." I sigh. "And a keeper."

"I'm so lucky," she whispers, eyeing Lee's back. "Damn, he works that suit, doesn't he?"

I nod, but my eyes are focused on the man standing on the other side of the pool.

Most of the guests huddle around the tables of hors d'oeuvres and standing heat lamps. Aiden stands alone, half-facing the valley, his face in profile to me. Even without his beard, I recognize him immediately.

"Excuse me," I say to no one as I walk in his direction.

"Hey." Landon steps in front of me. "We're on a date, right? Shouldn't we stick together?"

I blink myself out of my Aiden trance and focus on him. Over his shoulder, I spot our mothers standing together, smiling in our direction.

Thinking quickly, I wave at the two meddlers and then tell Landon, "Will you get us a plate of food? And if you're going to the bar, I'd love one of the signature cocktails. Thanks."

"Where are you going?" he asks as I walk away.

"I'm being polite and going to chat with your brother who appears to be here alone." As I speak, I barely glance over my shoulder at Landon.

My heels make a clicking sound on the hard surface around the pool, alerting Aiden to my approach.

When he turns to face me, his eyes trail up from my shoes to my shoulders before finally scanning my face. His lips curl into a wide grin. "You look beautiful. I thought women weren't supposed to show up the bride by looking better than she does?"

His compliment heats my skin. "You should consider wearing this suit all the time."

"Even on the river?" He laughs.

I touch the soft, smooth fabric covering his bicep. "Probably not. It might shrink and it would be a terrible crime to ruin something so perfect."

We're in a bubble for two, and the sounds of the party behind us fade as we stare at each other. At least we are until Landon comes stomping over with his hands full of drinks, precariously balancing plates on top of the glasses.

"I didn't bring you a drink, Aiden. Sorry." Landon's tone says he's not even a little bit apologetic.

"No problem. Already have a bourbon." Aiden holds up his glass. "Thanks."

With my cocktail in one hand and the small plate of food in the other, I stand awkwardly between the two of them as tension rolls off of their bodies.

"So this is lovely?" My voice lifts at the end, turning my statement into a question. "Beautiful evening for October with the view over the valley dotted with the yellow aspens. Did you notice the balloon trucks near the golf course? That's going to be beautiful on Sunday."

I can't keep this one-sided, boring monologue going forever.

Aiden catches my eye and smirks. "Should we talk about the weather? I hear there's a chance of light snow tonight at higher elevation."

Landon's attention flicks between the two of us. "Why are you discussing snow and trees?"

Aiden takes a sip of the brown liquid in his glass. "We're making polite conversation at a fancy event."

"You're being boring as fuck. I'm going to go find the bride and say hello." Landon shoves a mini slider into his mouth and follows it with the contents of his glass.

We remain silent until he's gone.

"I believe your date ditched you." Aiden drags his teeth over his bottom lip to fight his grin.

"It would appear I'm terribly boring." I meet his eyes, then giggle. "How are you?"

"I'm doing really well, and even better now that you're here." He keeps his voice low so only I can hear.

He's making all of the reasons I should resist him disappear with his charming words.

"Mind if we join you?" Sage steps beside me and tucks her arm under mine. "Hi, Aiden. You're a sharp dressed man tonight."

Lee hands her a glass of sparkling rosé. "Congrats on the big sale, Aiden. I read about it online this morning. I had no idea you were one of the founders of 8K Tech."

Aiden holds his glass up to his mouth to take a sip, but doesn't. He's frozen. "Uh, thanks."

My eyes bug out. "Put it in reverse, Lee. What did you just say?"

Lee's dark brows knit together. "Was my accent too thick?"

"You barely have an accent anymore." I wave him off and focus on Aiden, who is looking a hella lot more uncomfortable than he did a few minutes ago. "You sold your company?"

"Not the entire thing. Only my third, and I've stepped down as CEO." He finally takes a swallow of bourbon. "Guess the cat's out of the bag now."

"Oh, no. This isn't your average house cat. This is opening a sandwich bag and having a lion escape." I sound like Mara with the cat analogies. If she were here, I'm sure she'd come up with some better ones than I can.

Aiden shoots me a small smile. "Guess I need to come clean."

"Do tell," Sage encourages him.

"I like to compare it to summiting a mountain. My goal was to start a company and make it successful. I accomplished that and it was time to walk away. Mountaineers don't linger around the peak being smug. They climb down and move on to their next challenge. The time was right for me to do something different." He shrugs like it's no big deal, when in fact this is all a very big deal.

"I love it." Sage grins at him.

I'm too stunned to speak.

Aiden dips his head down to stare into my eyes. "Mae?"

"Congratulations," I mumble, without the enthusiasm he deserves.

"Are you okay?" Sage whispers, nudging me with her elbow.

"You're not broke?" I find my voice.

Aiden shakes his head. "No, why would you think that?"

"Because you were crashing at Landon's. I assumed you were desperate and out of options." My words sound judgmental to my own ears.

"And why would I be desperate?" He smiles at me, amused.

"Because of your addiction issues," I mutter, feeling embarrassed to bring it up in front of Lee and Sage.

Aiden's eyebrows lift toward his hairline. "Hold on, is this why you thought I was in rehab?"

"Now I'm confused," Sage says. "I think this is a conversation best had between the two of you. We'll go stand over there. I think I saw Zoe and Justin."

Lee follows behind her, glancing over his shoulder once, probably to make sure Aiden's safe from me and my assumptions.

"So?" Aiden leans his back against the railing, crosses his arms, and waits.

"Landon made it seem like your life was a mess and you walked away from your life to go find yourself. The words he used . . . I read between the lines."

"What are my addictions?" His full lips curve with a slight smirk. Now that his beard's gone, his exposed mouth seems almost vulgar.

I stare behind his shoulder at the valley and the twinkling of lights from the houses below us.

"Mae? I'm not mad at you. Tell me." He brushes his fingers along the back of my hand.

Taking a big inhale, I prepare myself to meet his eyes. What I find there is nothing but openness and curiosity, no judgment or anger. "At first I thought drugs or alcohol."

"At first?" His lips twitch with amusement.

"Gambling and Russian escorts were also in the running." I shove the words out of my mouth as quickly as possible and stare over his shoulder again.

He laughs and I cringe.

"Mae, look at me." His voice is commanding but soft.

I obey and manage not to squirm.

"Having an existential crisis and going on a long walk are dull and boring by comparison. I'm sorry to disappoint you."

"You're not a disappointment. I am." Movement across the pool catches my eye. People are slowly walking inside for dinner. "We should go. Everyone is sitting down and we'll be missed."

"Wait." Gripping my wrist, he stops me from leaving. "I'm not letting you walk away thinking you've disappointed me. Because you haven't."

"You should be mad I believed it possible you needed to go to rehab for five months because of your drug, alcohol, gambling, and kinky, paid sex addiction." A woman across the pool pauses and stares at me like she heard every word. If so, I've just started a crazy rumor about Aiden. Add it to my list of crimes.

"I'm not mad at you. Out of habit, I blame Landon for not telling you the truth about why I moved back, but it wasn't up to him to share my story." He gently strokes my wrist, and I feel the echo of his touch move through my blood stream.

"Margaret?" My mother's voice carries over to us from the entrance. "Are you joining us? Your date is already seated."

"Let's hop the fence and get out of here." Aiden jerks his head toward the stone wall with a ten foot drop.

I peer over the side. "We'd break a leg or ankle."

"Might. Or we could land safely and hightail it away." He quickly raises his eyebrows.

"Margaret?" My mother repeats my name, clearly annoyed I'm loitering.

Although I'm tempted, I want to avoid pissing off my family. "Later? We can escape when the party shifts to the concert."

"Deal." Using our distance and angle to his advantage, he gives me a soft kiss at the corner of my mouth.

For all she knows, he's whispering something in my ear.

She remains flanking the door like a guard at a palace, stoic and unsmiling until we get closer.

"Aiden."

Calling her tone cold is a compliment.

"Mrs. London, you look lovely this evening." He extends his hand to shake hers.

Margaret London can't abide bad manners so she allows him to take her hand. "I didn't realize you were still in town."

Translation: Her grapevine of gossips has failed to inform her. Heads will roll.

"Mae, Landon is already seated at your table. I believe you're at number nine. Aiden, there's an empty seat at table fifteen."

Translation: Don't plan on crashing my daughter's date with your brother.

"Thank you for saving me the trouble of finding a seat. I believe I'm a last minute addition. Mae, I appreciate our conversation. We'll have to continue it another time." He gives me a warm smile and walks away.

Translation: Your mother hates me and I'm going to leave now before she sprains a Botox frozen muscle trying to scowl at me.

The last part might be my own personal interpretation of his words.

"Shall we?" Mom steps beside me. "It isn't polite to leave your date and spend the night talking to another man."

"Aiden is his brother." And the far better option, but I keep this new knowledge to myself.

SIXTEEN

AIDEN

SWEEPING MY PALM over my freshly shaved cheek, I feel both naked and like I'm wearing a disguise. In my charcoal suit, I guess I am in a costume. The fit is tighter in the shoulders from hiking and paddling this summer. I brush a hand over the fine wool and take a moment to settle into my skin. Inhaling, I button my jacket and then straighten the cuffs of my shirt. This man isn't who I am anymore, but the people inside of the ballroom don't care. They'll see the expensive suit and well-groomed face, and come to their own conclusions.

News of the sale hit the business news cycle yesterday afternoon. So far no one has made a big deal out of my new financial status, other than Lee bringing it up in front of Sage. Would be nice if that continued through the weekend, but I'm not delusional enough to believe it will.

I pass table nine and notice two empty chairs.

"Aren't you joining us?" Sage asks, pointing to a seat between herself and Mae.

"Mrs. London pointed me to number fifteen." I pause, trying to locate my seat for the meal.

"That's the kids' table." Zoe points to the corner. "She must not like you."

"I'd rather sit at the kiddie one," Landon complains.

"We could switch," I suggest. "People still get us confused."

Mae snorts into her hand. "Not likely."

At the front of the room, a man stands and clinks his spoon against his glass, drawing everyone's attention. The crowd quiets and I realize I'm the only person standing.

Not wanting to be impolite, I slide into the seat next to Mae. "Guess I'm sitting here."

"It's about time we stood up to Margaret London, overlord of none." Mae's eyes dance with mischief. In her black outfit, she's a beautiful, dark flower.

Landon laughs a little too loud at something the speaker says. "Man, I wish I could see Twyla's face right now. I bet she's shitting herself."

Mae twists to face him. "Why? What did I miss?"

"Apparently, that's Topher's father and he just mentioned their pre-nup. Way to ruin the romance of the evening." Landon chuckles into his water glass. "So much for true love."

"Doesn't seem unreasonable, given the family fortunes at play and the young age of the couple." I think it's a good idea.

"I agree," Sage says.

Lee's eyes dart to her. "Would you want me to sign one?"

"No, never." Her eyes crinkle when she touches his cheek. Clearly, they're deeply in love.

"What about you?" Mae asks, tucking her napkin on her lap.

"Sign a pre-nup?" I ask, turning my back to Landon.

"Require your future wife to sign one," she says quietly. "Given you're worth millions."

"Who's got millions in the bank?" Landon interrupts us, leaning forward with his arm draped around Mae's shoulder. "Aiden? Yeah right."

Her eyes widen and she mouths, "He doesn't know?"

I flatten my lips together. "We'll talk about it later."

"I love the pool here," Sage changes the subject.

"Do you use the sun deck?" Grateful, I take the bait.

Mae giggles and Zoe bites her lip before saying, "Um, we prefer to swim at night."

My conversation with Landon and Easley pops into my head. Images of Mae naked and wet in the jacuzzi play like a slideshow. I've seen her in a bathing suit. It isn't that difficult to make the jump between that and her fully nude. A few mysteries remain and I plan to solve them as soon as possible.

We manage to avoid all talk of me and money for the three course meal and endless speeches. If it weren't for the concert at nine, I suspect we'd be in this room all night—or eternity, whichever comes first.

"I'm going to hit the head," Landon declares as we leave the banquet room. "Wait for me, Mae."

"I need to say hello to my parents. If we miss each other, I'll see you tomorrow." She stands on her toes, searching the people milling around the hotel.

"Want me to wait with you?" I ask her, reluctant to leave her side.

"I'll just be a minute. Oh, there they are, talking with your parents. We can both play dutiful children together." She rolls her eyes. "Let's get this over with."

"Aiden," Mom greets me with a hug. "It's so good to see you. And Mae, how lovely you look in all black."

I chuckle, my shoulders shaking at the compliment. Gwendolyn does love funeral appropriate attire.

"What's so funny?" Mae asks with her head cocked to the side.

"Later. I'm going to go find Landon. Be right back." Wanting to kiss her or squeeze her hand, and knowing I can't break the charade of the evening, I give her a small wave before walking away.

Public restrooms are located down a long hall off of the

main lobby, opposite the entrance. The hall is empty as is the men's room when I open the door. I even call out Landon's name and check the stalls. *Strange.* Doubting he'd ditch Mae after all of his posturing this evening, I exit and loiter in the narrow hall to pull out my phone. I'll text him to meet us at the concert. Pausing in the quiet space, I hear voices and a woman's laughter coming from behind the door to the family bathroom next to me. Like a creeper, I step closer and confirm the man's voice sounds like Landon.

That little shit.

I bet he's in there with the bartender he was flirting with earlier. Pissed on Mae's behalf, I shove the door, surprised it's unlocked and swings open.

Twyla screams and jumps away from my brother, who is sporting a lovely shade of rose lipstick now.

"Don't you knock?" He straightens to his full height and broadness.

"That's your issue with me walking in on you kissing the bride at her rehearsal dinner?" I shout at him.

Twyla pleads, "Please don't say anything to Topher or my parents. Please. I had . . . a momentary urge to see what I might be missing. Now it's over and I'd die if anyone finds out."

"Not my place to tell anyone." I glare at my brother, not for the first time wishing we didn't share the same blood.

With another promise that the kiss was moment of bad decision making, Twyla slips through the door behind me. In case anyone is loitering in the hall, I turn the lock so we're not discovered inside of the single bathroom she left. Talk about scandal. Caught with one of us would be terrible, but both of us? None of us would ever live it down.

"This is fucked up even for you," I tell him, keeping my voice low enough we're not overheard, but loud enough to convey my disgust.

"You know I've always had a thing for Twyla. Way before Mae. I had to take my shot before it was too late." He checks his face in the mirror and then removes the lipstick with a paper towel.

"Do you love her?" I'm pissed off and disgusted, but if they love each other, then we're dealing with a whole other kind of mess.

"I don't know." He shrugs, and I want to punch him.

"You'd know if you did. This isn't a fucking maybe situation. Lives and reputations are at stake." I practically spit out the words.

"You sound like Mom. Who cares about other people's opinions? Why give a fuck what some aunt or cousin or neighbor has to say? Doesn't fucking matter."

"Then what are we doing here? If you don't care, why all the shenanigans with Mae?"

"Unfinished business." He juts his chin out.

"She doesn't owe you anything. Didn't when you were teenagers and doesn't now. Is that all this was? Getting her into bed? What happened to becoming a decent man?"

"I wanted to try another tactic. Turns out I do better with women when I'm an asshole. Although, I think Mae talking me up helped push Twyla in my direction. I should thank her, and I guess you, too." He moves to step around me, but I shift to block him.

"I'm not done yet. Did you hint to Mae I went to rehab? For what? To make yourself look better? Low, even for you."

"Come on, Mr. CEO. Didn't you learn this in business that sometimes to make yourself seem better, you had to knock down your competition in the eyes of your targets?" His smile is smug and unrepentant.

"Only if you don't believe in your own product. Otherwise, it's better to focus on the positive." Little Shit isn't going to turn this back on me.

"I think we've been in here long enough. Let's go outside, go to the concert, and enjoy the rest of the night." His smooth tone reminds me of the snake in *The Jungle Book*.

"Fuck off," I spit.

"You don't want me to tell Mae how it was your words in the text and how you were willing to deceive her into thinking I'm a good guy. Might ruin your own shot to fuck her."

I don't punch him, but I do shove him into the wall. "Leave her out of it."

"Happy to. You don't tell anyone about Twyla, I keep your secret. Sounds like a fair deal, don't you think?" He pushes my arm away and stands, smoothing out the creases in his shirt.

I don't know how Mae's going to react when she finds out. All I know is I want her to hear it from me—not Landon's version.

Her concerned eyes scan my face. "Everything okay? You two were gone a long time. The gang left a few minutes ago to save us a spot."

"Having a brotherly chat, catching up on life." Landon grins at the Londons. "Ready for some Lionel Ritchie?"

Mae's mother claps her hands and bounces on her toes. "Can't wait."

Who knew Margaret was a super fan? And who knew Mr. Ritchie would play a wedding rehearsal dinner? I guess anything is possible with the right amount of money.

Acting as if nothing happened, Landon commandeers one of the carts and has Mae sit up front with him. Her parents take the middle row, and I hop on the back, facing away from the rest. I'm not sure I could stomach having to look at my brother's face right now.

The night air is cool, hinting at future snows. Mae and her mother both have wraps around their shoulders and blankets tucked around their legs.

We're among the last to arrive and the band is already warming up on stage when we locate the rest of Mae's friends. I spread out another blanket and sit next to Lee, away from the main group. Mae gives me a funny look before claiming a spot near Zoe. Of course, LS sits right next to Mae after giving me a shit-eating grin.

People scream and shout when they hear the opening notes of "All Night Long."

"Nothing against Lionel, but anyone else think this is a little weird?" Lee asks the group.

"I heard a woman, who might be Mrs. Tierney, telling her friend the whole family are huge fans. This is their gift to Topher," Justin explains, leaning around Zoe.

"This is a thing with wealthy people?" Zoe asks him, and then turns to Sage. "Private concerts? Because if it is, I'd like to put in a request for Ed Sheeran."

Sage rolls her eyes while Justin laughs and tugs Zoe against his side. "Duly noted, sweetheart."

Observing the group and how Mae's surrounded by couples, I wonder how much that influenced her decision to agree to the date with Landon. It's clear from her body language she wants nothing to do with him. That's a relief.

Closer to stage, a few couples dance or sway to the music. The small crowd cheers when the bride and groom start dancing to "Hello."

I've never really listened to the lyrics, but in this moment, watching Landon watch Twyla, they seem bizarrely appropriate.

Lionel Ritchie is singing the soundtrack to our lives.

After their dance, Twyla and Topher weave through the crowd, stopping to say hello and thank you to their guests.

Mae hugs her cousin and compliments her on her dress.

Topher shakes my hand and introduces himself.

"Thanks for letting me crash the dinner and this concert," I tell him.

"You're welcome." He's polite and stoic. The opposite of my brother.

"Landon, it's good to see you." Twyla turns her cheek for my brother to kiss.

He rests his hand on her shoulder, and after pressing his lips to her skin, whispers something in her ear. If I weren't standing next to them, I would probably miss the blush that spreads across her cheeks and down her neck.

"I'm going to head back to my hotel room at the Jerome for some beauty rest. Have a wonderful time. Enjoy the rest of the concert." Twyla smiles at us.

"You leaving, too, Topher?" Landon asks the groom.

Topher shakes his head. "No, I'll be here until the bitter end. I'm escorting Twyla to the car."

Strange phrasing to describe one of the best nights of his life.

"You don't want to miss your special concert." Landon pats Topher's shoulder. "I'm leaving too. I'd be happy to make sure Twyla makes it to the car safely."

"That's nice of you." Topher flashes a small fraction of a smile.

The little shit just made his move right in front of the groom. I don't know if I should be impressed or outraged, and decide on a combination of both.

"Aiden, can you make sure Mae gets home safely?" Landon grins at me like a shark. "Mae, you don't mind, do you? I'll pick you up for the wedding tomorrow afternoon."

Not aware of the larger game being played, Mae's shoulders relax with relief at his offer. "That's fine with me if Aiden is okay with it."

"Of course. It would be the gentlemanly thing to do." I shoot daggers at Landon.

Ignoring me, he holds out his elbow for Twyla to take. "I'm always a gentleman. Good night, everyone."

Sage makes a small gagging noise in her throat.

When Landon and Twyla leave, Topher returns to his friends and family near the stage.

Bile burns the back of my throat. "I think I'm going to call it a night, too. Mae, are you ready?"

She nods and stands, dragging the blanket wrapped around her shoulders with her. "Never been more ready."

We say our goodbyes and walk toward the drop off area.

"Didn't you say you were staying at the Viceroy?" she asks, wrapping her arm around my bicep.

Her warmth and proximity are a balm on the burn of my anger. "I do. Want me to invite you upstairs for a night cap?"

"I thought you'd never ask." She leans closer and kisses the corner of my jaw.

In the grand scheme of the lies and misdeeds of tonight, mine pale in comparison. Reassuring myself my actions were done from a place of good, I decide the truth can wait for another day.

SEVENTEEN

MAE

AS WE SLOWLY drive down hill to the Viceroy, I place my hand on the back of his neck and rub. "What's wrong?"

"Nothing," he grits out between his teeth.

"Is it the thought of driving me home to Aspen? I can get a car. Or text Sage to pick me up after the concert." I fumble in my small clutch to find my phone.

"Stop. It isn't you."

"Are you about to give me the 'it isn't you, it's me' speech?" My stomach drops. "I'm sorry for thinking you were an addict."

His lips curve with a smile. "A kinky sex addict."

My cheeks flush. "I can't believe I shared that. For the record, I never fully explored what your kink might be."

"Hmm. That's something we might have to discover together." His voice dips lower, becoming rougher, and turning my insides into melted marshmallows.

A soft moan escapes my mouth as I press my thighs together. This man will ruin me for all others, of this I am certain. Unlike—

"Did something happen in the bathroom when you went to find Landon?" I ask, unable to give up my quest for the truth.

"Sometimes, you're too perceptive for your own good. Trust me, this isn't about you." He blows out a long exhale. "My brother is an asshole, and for reasons I can't say right now I'm unable to say more."

His smile is apologetic and his eyes hold genuine regret.

"If I'm so perceptive, maybe you can give me a clue, and then if I figure out what's going on without you telling me, you won't be breaking your promise to Landon."

He releases a weak chuckle. "If I ask you to let it go, at least for tonight, would you?"

"Pretend your brother doesn't exist? Consider it done." I grin at him. "So tell me, what was it like growing up an only child?"

This earns a genuine laugh from him as he swings the cart through the hotel entrance and then parks it.

"What floor is your room on?" I ask as we stroll through the lobby toward the elevator bank.

"I have an apartment here." He stops in front of an open elevator marked 'Residences.'

He slips a keycard from his suit pocket and presses it against the scanner before hitting the button for the fifth floor. Not the penthouse level, but one floor below.

I practice keeping my face neutral as I stare ahead at the doors closing.

"Nice," I finally manage to say when we exit into a tastefully decorated hallway.

"It's only temporary until I can find the right place." He leads the way to his door.

"Because you're now a multi-millionaire several times over?" I fail to keep the excitement out of my voice.

"How do you know that?"

"I snuck into the bathroom earlier and found the article on Google." I don't bother to feel sheepish. "You're not a slacker at all. You know what this makes you?"

He laughs, opening the door and allowing me to enter in front of him. Lights flicker to life in the stylish living room. "What am I?"

"You're a poser. A fake. A fraud." I lean against his kitchen island.

"I'm none of those things." He stalks toward me, all strength and reserved power. "Just me. Same Aiden, only more myself than I've been in years."

Anticipation makes my skin tingle with each step he takes closer to me. "I like this Aiden."

Caging me against the island, he braces his arms close to my sides. "Good, because I like you, too."

My breath quivers when I try to inhale deeply.

With a swift movement, he lifts me up to the counter. I gasp in surprise. Before I can say anything, his mouth crashes against my lips, and his tongue finds mine as he claims my mouth. Losing myself in the kiss, I roam my hands over his chest, shoving his suit jacket off of his shoulders and then undoing the buttons of his shirt. His hand cups and squeezes my breast through my jumpsuit, drawing out a soft moan from me when he rolls a nipple between his fingers.

I part my legs for him and he steps closer until his hips grind against mine. Through the thin fabric of his suit pants, the ridge of his hard cock rubs against my core. On instinct, I begin rocking against him, seeking the friction I crave.

His fingers skim over my sides as he murmurs against my lips, "How do you get out of this beautiful contraption?"

"Hidden zipper on the back." I move to undo it myself, but his hand stops me.

"Let me." Leaning down, he presses a kiss against the swell of my breast through the silk fabric and then drags the zipper down with his hand. When the fabric parts and drapes over my shoulder, he gently pulls it away from my body, leaving my breasts exposed.

"So beautiful," he whispers as he kisses one breast and then the other, alternating between cupping them with his hand and lavishing them with his mouth.

The combination of his words and touch sends a rush of pleasure through my body. I need him. Now, if sooner isn't possible.

Refocusing on his buttons, I get the shirt open and drop it to the floor next to his jacket. He's still wearing too many clothes, but I savor the feel of his chest beneath my fingertips. Every inch of him is covered with hard muscle. My fingers skim down the smooth skin of his biceps and then back up to trail over his pecs before dropping down to his abs, which bunch and tighten beneath my touch.

His mouth finds mine again and he's savage with his kiss, as desperate as I feel. Too soon he pulls away and drops to his knees in front of me.

There are moments in life I'll never forget. Seeing Aiden kneeling before me, his eyes hooded with lust, is one of them.

With a tug, he removes the bottom half of my jumpsuit and drags my underwear down in the same movement. I kick off my heels.

"What are you doing?" I ask, hoping I know exactly what he's about to do.

A devilish smirk twists his mouth. "As if you don't know."

Rising on his knees, he kisses a line from my ankle to the top of my thigh. I arch my back and try to direct him to where I ache for him.

"Lie back and let me take care of you." He presses his hand on my stomach. "I have you."

I rest my lower back against the cool, quartz surface, but lift up on my bent elbows. Because if Aiden Roberts is going down on me, I need to watch. If this only happens once, I need to have a visual to remember the moment.

Pressing his hands on my inner thighs, he encourages me to open for him. Between licks and kisses, he keeps telling me how beautiful and sexy I am. When he hums against my clit, my back arches. I'm so close so fast, it's a little embarrassing.

"Don't hold back," he whispers, meeting my eyes as he slips a finger inside of me.

I try to keep my eyes open, but my lids keep fluttering closed with each new wave of pleasure.

"You're so fucking sexy. I've wanted to do this forever." He adds another finger and presses both against the front of my inner walls before tonguing my clit again.

"Oh, oh, Aiden," I shout as my orgasm slams into me in one huge rush of sensation. Everything else in the world disappears besides his touch and the pleasure pulsing through my body.

He brings me back to reality with a soft kiss to my inner thigh. When he slides his fingers out of my body, I miss the contact instantly. Crawling over me, he kisses a path from my navel to my neck, pausing to suck a nipple into his mouth.

"You are spectacular. Don't ever believe anything less," he whispers against my lips and then kisses me.

I kiss him back, not caring that I can taste myself on his lips. If anything, the combination of his minty mouth and my own scent flips a switch inside of me. I'm greedy for more of him.

"Do you own a bed?" I ask, tipping his chin up with my finger.

"Of course." He smirks. "Want to see it?"

Not waiting for me to confirm, he slides his hands underneath me and lifts me off of the counter. "Wrap your legs around my hips."

Kissing me, he walks us down the hall and then drops me on his bed. I gaze up at him while he kicks off his shoes, undoes his buckle, and slides his pants and underwear to the floor.

He stands naked in all his glorious beauty and I've never seen anything sexier than when he strokes his cock while ravishing me with his eyes.

"If we don't have sex soon, I might combust." My skin burns, and despite having an orgasm less than five minutes ago, I ache for him to be inside of me.

"We can't have spontaneous combustion, can we?" He opens the nightstand drawer and takes a condom out.

"Please tell me you have more than one," I whisper, mostly as a quiet prayer.

"It's a brand new box. Will that be enough?" He doesn't hide the amusement in his voice.

"For now." I watch as he gives his swollen head a tug before sliding on the latex. Condoms are weird and unsexy unless it's Aiden sheathing himself with one in order to have sex with me. Then it's the sexiest fucking thing I've ever seen in my life.

"This isn't going to be slow and gentle," he warns me with a low growl. "At least not the first time."

When he settles between my legs, I wrap my arms around his back and kiss him, losing myself in the sensation of his tongue stroking mine as he thrusts into me in one long stroke.

Even after the incredible orgasm he gave me as a warm up, it takes my body a moment to adjust to his size. He switches to shallow thrusts, kissing me and thumbing my clit. The combination sends me racing toward another orgasm, but I need more.

"Harder, please," I beg, unashamed to ask for what I need.

He complies, giving me deep, strong thrusts that hit the spot inside of me.

"That. Don't stop," I whisper.

"Not until you come again." He grinds his hips against mine, as deep as he can possibly be.

I explode and tighten around him, pulsing waves of pleasure washing over me once again.

"Sexiest thing ever," he whispers as I come down from my second orgasm. "I want you to go for three, but I'm not going to last."

Changing positions so he's kneeling with my ankle on his shoulder, his movements speed up, losing their rhythm right before he stills, arching his back as he comes with a deep growl.

When his orgasm fades, he leans over me and kisses me. "You are amazing."

After another quick peck, he leaves the bed to clean up.

I stretch, feeling sore in places I've forgotten about, but completely sated and happy.

He returns with a warm wash cloth for me, carefully and lovingly cleaning me. "Bathroom's all yours. Fresh toothbrushes under the sink."

I kiss him and then roll myself off of the bed. "Can I borrow a T-shirt to sleep in?"

"Top drawer to the left in the closet."

Naked, I pad across the room, feeling the weight of his stare on my back.

Aiden is nothing what I expected and everything I fantasized he'd be.

EIGHTEEN

MAE

WEARING AN ANCIENT pair of jeans, a faded Colorado T-shirt, and a pair sneakers, Aiden insists on escorting me downstairs.

I repay the favor by insisting on making out with him during the short elevator ride to the lobby.

"Last chance to ditch it all and stay with me instead . . ." He presses his lips against mine once, twice more. "Say the word and we'll lock ourselves in the apartment and order room service. No one knows my apartment number and won't be able to find us for hours even if they organize a search party."

"Stop making me laugh so I can give you a proper kiss goodbye. It's impossible to kiss and smile at the same time." I prove this point by attempting to do both at the same time.

"I'm sure with practice, we'll tackle this weakness." His arms wind around my waist and he kisses me thoroughly, sweeping his tongue against mine. *Master kisser extraordinaire.*

A polite cough alerts us to company. It appears in our horny fog, we've stopped in front of the elevators and are blocking access.

An older woman in a smart leisurewear ensemble smiles

knowingly at us. "Nothing like young love."

I open my mouth to correct her assumption, but Aiden beats me too it by saying, "Thank you. I couldn't agree more."

As the doors close, she basks in the beauty of his smile like a cat in the sun. I can't blame her. I feel the same way when he directs the full force of his handsomeness and charms in my direction.

"Why are you grinning?" His breath tickles my ear when he speaks.

"You made that woman's day." My grin widens.

"Did I? I didn't notice." He stares into my eyes and it feels like he can see all the way through me to my soul.

"I have a vague memory of plans for today, but can't remember what they are." I back him toward the elevators.

He smirks at me. "I changed my mind. We're going together. Landon can go by himself."

"I love the way you think." I stretch up to show my appreciation for his brain with a kiss, which I end with a slight nip of his bottom lip. I might have a small obsession forming over it and I have zero regrets.

"I'll pick you up at two." He sweeps his lips over mine one more time.

I manage to break away from him and take a couple of steps in the direction of the exit before he calls my name.

Thinking he's changed his mind, I grin at him when I turn around. "Yes?"

"This is a little awkward, but I don't know where you live, nor do I have your cell number. I basically have no way of contacting you other than through your work."

A couple getting off of the elevator overhears this exchange and snickers. They seem vaguely familiar to me, but I don't know their names. Could be guests from last night. Feeling the need to clarify this situation and redeem myself in their eyes, I clear my throat and clearly enunciate, "I'm not a Russian escort. In case you were wondering. He's not paying me for sex or companionship."

Aiden fails at containing his deep rumble laughter. "We're all good. You're not cops, are you?"

My eyes bug out of my head.

Thankfully, the couple laughs as they walk away. She twists her head to glance at us over her shoulder. "Ah, young love."

A sweet sentiment, but I'm confused if she believes this is a modern day *Pretty Woman* moment. We are standing in a hotel lobby and I'm obviously wearing last night's clothes. Or overdressed for Saturday morning errands in my black jumpsuit and heels.

"And on that note, I'm leaving."

"Phone, please." He holds out his hand, his shoulders still shaking with laughter.

Obeying his command, I pass him my phone.

"All set. I texted you some emojis so you know it's me." Grinning, he hands me back the phone. "See you at two."

The closing elevator doors swallow him before I can ask about the emojis. Glancing at my phone, I see he's sent me nothing but red hearts.

ᛋᚱᚴ

He didn't use the word ravish, but I'm going to assume that's his motivation.

Two o'clock on the dot, my door buzzer rings. Pressing the button on the video monitor, Aiden's handsome face fills the screen. I pause for a moment to admire him in his deep navy suit and open-collared white shirt. He's clean shaven again today, and while I do love direct access to his mouth, I kind of miss his beard and scraggly appearance. There was something wild about him that's been tamed by custom tailored wool and a smooth face.

Several seconds later, he arrives at my open door, where

I'm casually leaning against the jamb.

"You look incredible." He sweeps his gaze from my loose waves, over the silky green, maxi dress hugging my curves down to my nude booties.

I'd planned to wear heels, but we did get a light dusting of snow overnight. Nothing to stick on the roads or grassy surfaces down here, but the tops of the mountains have a sprinkling of white that hasn't melted yet.

With the sun out and the sky a crystalline sapphire, the day is perfect for a wedding.

"Stop looking at me like you want to eat me," I tell him.

"Why? Maybe that's exactly what I want to do." He crosses the threshold and steps closer to me. "I walk you back to the arm of the couch and have you sit. Then I could lift up your skirt, carefully so as not to wrinkle the fabric before kneeling in front of you, slipping aside the lace or silk covering you, baring you for me. Maybe I'll linger there for a moment, memorizing your delicate skin, how it thickens and swells with desire. Unable to resist any longer, I'll sweep my tongue up your center, tasting and enjoying every second, every moan and sigh of your pleasure."

My legs give out and I sit heavily on the arm of the couch before slipping down to the cushions.

"Someone needs to text Twyla and tell her we're going to be late." Pulling him forward by his jacket lapels, I kiss the hell out of him, not caring if he rumples his suit or my dress.

He moves his mouth down my jaw to the tender skin by my ear, his warm breath tickling my skin and making me squirm. "I somehow doubt the bride has access to her phone and is responding to text messages."

"You make a fair point. We'll have to send our regrets later." I smooth my hands down his back before cupping his waist and then his ass. Being a mountain girl, I never considered myself the type of woman who goes gaga over a man in a suit. Turns out I'd never seen the right man in the right suit before.

"Why are you desperate to get out of going to this wedding? Other than Landon is your official plus one." Standing, he lifts me up by my arms. Once we're both vertical, he steps back, sweeping his hands down my dress to smooth out any wrinkles. Every touch makes me feel cared for and important.

Pausing for second because I've never given it much thought, I try to come up with a reason. "Honestly, I'm not sure. I didn't want to go even before the set up. Big, pretentious, family events annoy me. Twyla is younger than I am and getting married, not that age matters. All of my friends are paired off like we're loading up a new ark. My mother is obsessed with weddings and who is getting married versus who isn't, which makes me feel like I have an expiration date stamped on my forehead."

Turns out, I have a lot of issues around weddings.

With a sheepish smile, I duck my head and stare out the window at the yellow aspen leaves.

"Those are all valid points." Cupping my cheek, he stands in front of me and gives me a soft, lingering kiss. "However, we should make an appearance at least. We can duck out early."

"I considered developing a sudden case of Whooping Cough to avoid going." I wrinkle my nose at how silly I'm being about the whole event. It's a few hours of my life I'll never get back, but so what? I'll never have those hours I wasted on researching rare contagious diseases again either.

"You're ridiculous." He picks up my coat and small purse.

"Why do you say it like this is a good thing?" I allow him to slip my coat over my shoulders.

"Because you are the best thing to happen to me."

NINETEEN

MAE

EVERYONE LOOKS GORGEOUS and fancy, like we're going to adult prom in the middle of the afternoon.

Zoe arches an eyebrow at my date. "Did you upgrade your Roberts brother?"

"What happened to Landon? Is he locked in a closet somewhere?" Grinning, Sage appears delighted by the idea.

"Is this approved by your mother?" Mara giggles.

I answer all of their questions in order. "Yes. I don't know because he has apparently ditched me. Most definitely not approved and I don't care."

Our turn to board comes, and we squeeze together in the gondola. Wrapping his arms around my waist, Aiden presses his front against my back while we enjoy the views during the ascent.

At the top, we disembark into a long line of open-sided but heated tents. A calm woman—with the voice of a patient pre-school teacher—instructs us to leave our coats at the coat check before moving along. Elegant heat towers line the path to the seating area in front of a huge arch covered with white and pale blush roses, birch branches, and clumps of silvery greens with gold gold accents. Beyond the flat area, the slope drops into the valley below. Snow dusted peaks surround us, creating an incredible backdrop. This view will never get old.

"It's perfect," I whisper before catching myself.

A blonde cellist plays softly from her chair off to the side of the altar. We're greeted with waiters holding trays of champagne and sparkling water.

"Your cousin went all out, didn't she?" Mara asks, holding a flute and twisting her head to take in every detail.

"It's the wedding of the year," I mumble, scanning the crowd for Landon and my parents. "Anyone see Landon?"

"I'll go find my mother and ask her." Aiden walks away, winding through the crowd.

"Spill everything," Zoe demands. "Quick before he comes back or Landon shows up."

"Save the details for Taco Tuesday," Mara suggests, "when we have more time for the good stuff."

"Aiden and I are together as of last night. It's been building since the raft trip, maybe even the night at the museum." I give them the very basics.

"I knew you'd find a better date." Sage squeezes my arm. "Everything works out as it should."

Aiden returns, flanked by both of our mothers, who wear matching perturbed expressions.

"Found them," he says with a flash of a smile.

"Where's your date?" Mom asks me.

I point to Aiden. "Right there."

Mrs. Roberts sighs. "She means Landon. You were in charge of him."

"I was?" I ask, confused. "No one told me."

My mother's sigh is even more exasperated. "You had one job, Mae. To keep Landon distracted."

I glance at my friends and their boyfriends to confirm I'm

not the only one lost in this conversation.

Aiden rests a hand on my waist. "Apparently, at the request of your aunt, our mothers were in cahoots before the bridal shower."

"Aunt Cecily wanted me to be Landon's date? Why?" I stare at my mother.

"She knew you two had a thing in high school and figured your long history meant you could deal with him," Mom explains.

"Why the elaborate scheming?" Aiden asks, sounding amused.

"Apparently," my mother lowers her voice, "there was concern about Landon's behavior given his feelings for Twyla."

My eyebrows can't crawl any higher on my face. "Landon has feelings?"

Beside me, Sage snorts.

The cello music switches to the prelude for Bach's first Cello Suite as uniformed staff encourage people to take their seats.

Our mothers give me one last frown of disapproval before finding their seats.

"Can you believe this? I was hired to be a babysitter for your brother?" I laugh, expecting Aiden to join me. "Unpaid, too."

He doesn't even crack a smile. Instead, he pulls out his phone and makes a call.

I can hear the ringing on the other end, and then Landon's voicemail message. "What's happening?"

"Either nothing and Landon's late. Or we're about to witness the scandal of the year." Aiden's mouth is set in a grim line. "Shall we sit?"

Perplexed by his vague answer, I allow him to guide me to a row of seats near the back.

Once we're settled, I twist in my chair to face him. "Spill."

He holds a finger up to his mouth. "Later. The groom has arrived."

Topher stands to the right of the altar, looking as bland as ever despite wearing an elegant tuxedo. Beside him, his groomsmen fidget and shuffle their feet. After Mr. and Mrs. Tierney take their seats, my cousin, Ailey escorts his mother to her place in the front row. Twyla's bridesmaids do the step, together, step, together down the aisle.

It's all lovely and perfect with the sun shining down and small, puffy white clouds dotting the sky.

We all patiently wait for the music to shift to the first notes of "Here Comes the Bride." Instead, the cellist loops through another Cello Suite.

The gondola arrives and I cast a glance over my shoulder, expecting my uncle and Twyla to make a grand entrance.

I'm not the only one who's shocked when the doors open and my frazzled looking uncle steps out alone. A collective gasp sweeps through the guests.

In full panic mode, my aunt jumps out of her chair and dashes down the aisle. Topher and his parents follow quickly behind, joining my uncle at the gondola.

Two hundred sets of ears strain to hear their conversation.

The only word I can clearly make out is Landon.

Standing, Aiden swears and takes his phone out of his jacket pocket again. Hitting dial, he listens to it ring before voicemail picks up.

"What the fuck is going on?" Mara asks the question we're all thinking.

"We should go now before there's a huge line for the gondolas," Zoe suggests, completely serious. "There's not enough champagne on this mountain to smooth over this scandal."

I switch off airplane mode on my phone and try calling Landon, thinking maybe he'll speak to me if he won't take his brother's call.

It doesn't even ring, going straight to voicemail.

I try Twyla's number. Same.

"No," I gasp. "You don't think she left all this to run off with Landon, do you?"

"Why would she walk away from this perfect wedding?" Zoe echoes me.

Aiden stares at his phone.

Sage's face is a mask of confusion. "I can't believe anyone would choose Landon over a decent guy like Topher."

Lee drapes his arm around her shoulders. "Not all women come to their senses like you did."

"Wow. I didn't think the cocky little shit had balls to do something like this," Aiden mumbles, mostly to himself.

"Come on, people are starting to catch on and line up for the gondola. I don't want to get stuck on this mountain any longer than we need to." Zoe hurries down our row.

Mara makes a beeline for one of the waiters and speaks to him. He nods and leaves, returning a few seconds later with a case of champagne. Jesse laughs as she hands it to him.

"Don't judge me. This has all been paid for and it would be a shame if it wasn't enjoyed." Mara gives me a wink.

Zoe spies the box in Jesse's arms. "If we can take champagne, do you think we could swing by the Jerome and rescue some of the cake? There's probably an entire table full of cupcakes going to waste."

Justin kisses her temple. "We'll organize a rescue mission."

She grins at him and then says to the group, "Meet back at Sage and Lee's condos? They have the most room."

Everyone agrees with varying degrees of enthusiasm as we make our way toward the gondola.

"You know something, don't you?" I whisper so only Aiden can hear me.

With a solemn nod, he confirms what I've suspected since last night.

"Spill."

"I caught Landon and Twyla kissing in the bathroom at the

hotel," he says with a low voice, keeping his attention forward as we follow Zoe.

"No way," I gasp. "At her rehearsal dinner?"

He nods again. "Landon told me it was a last hurrah, but obviously he was lying."

"Do you think they really ran off together?" I still can't believe she'd choose him.

"Guess we'll have to wait and see. They'll turn up eventually." He presses his hand against my lower back to guide me onto the waiting gondola.

As the doors close, I catch my mother smiling at me from the line. At least she doesn't appear to be in a murderous snit anymore. I'm shocked when she gives me a thumbs-up and tilts her head toward Aiden.

Guess he's her favorite Roberts brother, too.

⚜

Landon's name appears in the text window on my home screen.

I show my phone to Aiden. "He's alive."

"Why is he texting you?" he asks, right before his phone pings with a new message.

"I don't know. This is all he's written." I shift closer to Aiden on the couch. We're still at Sage's condo. The rest of the gang are scattered around the room, some sprawled on the other end of the sectional or sitting on stools at the kitchen island. Multiple champagne bottles sit empty next to a half-eaten tray of cupcakes.

"Looks like he's started a group text." He opens up his messages.

"Should we write something or wait for him to say more?" I stare at the screen.

Aiden types something and then erases it. "Let's let him take the lead."

A few seconds later, dots appear, indicating Landon's typing.

"He needs to type faster." I stare at my screen, willing him to be using both thumbs and not pecking out each letter with one finger. No one has time for that.

Landon: *If anyone is looking for Twyla, tell them she's with me.*

Aiden: *And where are you?*

Landon: *Denver.*

Me: *You might want to stay there. Or go into hiding.*

Beside me, Aiden laughs.

Landon: *Yeah, I imagine people are pissed.*

Aiden: *A little.*

Landon: *It had to be done. I love her and she loves me.*

"Whoa," I say out loud.

Me: *You couldn't have figured this out before her wedding day to another man?*

Landon: *Yeah, my timing might suck.*

Me: *You think?*

"You're coming in hot." Aiden chuckles.

"His actions are selfish and hurtful." I defend my anger. "What about Topher in all of this? Completely humiliated in front of Aspen's finest. He probably won't be able to listen to Lionel Ritchie ever again. Landon has ruined one of his great joys as well as stolen his wife."

Landon: *Mae, you should know, anything Aiden did was because I asked him to. I think he cares for you, so don't be too mad at him.*

Aiden: *Shut up. Stop before you make things worse.*

"What's he talking about?" I face Aiden.

Blowing out a deep breath, he slips my phone from my hand. "You have every right to be mad, but try to remember you like me, and I like you. What's between us is real."

I glance around at my friends. I have a bad feeling about whatever he's going to say next. "I think we should take this conversation outside."

"Let's go back to your place and I'll explain everything." Standing, he holds out his hand to me.

"How bad is it?" I ask, refusing his gesture.

"Hopefully not as terrible as you're imagining." He gives me a small smile.

We say our goodbyes and walk down the path to the street.

"Tell me now." I stop when I reach the sidewalk.

He brushes his hand over his hair and then rests it on the back of his neck. "How familiar are you with *Cyrano*?"

"The book we had to read in high school?" I ask, wondering why he wants to discuss classic literature.

"You know the basic premise?"

And then it clicks. "The texts were from you?"

He nods. "Some of them. Not the ones involving eggplants and peaches."

"The champagne?" I ask, surprised and not surprised about the texts. The inconsistency of tone never made sense.

"My idea, but I made him pay for it." His brow crinkles with worry. "How mad are you?"

"I'm not sure." I rub my temples. "Why would you trick me?"

"A whole bunch of reasons, most of them stupid and embarrassing." He winces. "At first, I wanted to help Landon out, because he's my brother. Then I did it for you."

Scrunching up my face, I stare at him. "You wanted me to fall for Landon?"

"Never. Not after I saw you at the fundraiser. You deserve better than him. I knew you were stuck with him as your date, and I wanted to make it a better experience for you by trying to make him into a decent guy."

"By pretending to be him?" Several different emotions go to battle inside of my head. Anger, confusion, and hurt are winning right now.

"Only a few times. My coaching suggestions were mostly

ignored, as you can tell from your interactions with him. Despite my best efforts, I failed to improve his personality," he says, resigned. "I think the project was doomed from the start."

"Landon is hopeless." I smile in spite of the mixed emotions swirling inside of me.

"You don't hate me?" he asks, a nervous edge to his voice.

"I'm not not mad, but I could never hate you." I touch his hand. "Landon, on the other hand, is off the birthday party list."

Aiden chuckles. "You have a list of invites for your birthday parties?"

"It's more a figure of speech." The tension between us evaporates. I don't want to be mad at Aiden. Anger is a toxic emotion.

"I will make it up to you." Holding my hand, he slides his fingers between mine.

"How?" I know I'm going to forgive him, but I'm curious to hear his plans.

"I'm thinking lots of over-the-top romantic gestures intended to swoop you off your feet." He ducks his head to brush his lips over mine.

"Sounds kind of vague." I'm not going to let him off with some random promises.

With his mouth a few inches away from mine, he asks, "What are you doing tomorrow morning?"

"Is this your way of asking me to spend the night again? Maybe I need time alone to sulk and stew." I want to do neither of those things.

"My place is closer for what I have planned. We can stop by your condo for you to change and pack an overnight bag with some warm layers for tomorrow's surprise." His confidence returns, and damn if it isn't intoxicating.

"This so-called plan of yours doesn't involve a cold, watery death, does it? Because I'm not going rafting with you."

"No rafts. No water. Death is unlikely." He smirks and then kisses me before I can ask another snarky question. "Say yes. To my crazy plan. To forgiving me for being a sneaky bastard. Say yes to me."

"Yes."

TWENTY

AIDEN

SHE'S HERE AND willing to give me a chance. That's all that matters to me. I'll do whatever it takes to prove I'm worthy of her forgiveness and her heart.

As gorgeous as she looked in her flowy green dress earlier today, she's never more beautiful than when she's naked. I strip away her clothes as slowly as I can manage without losing my mind. Until I'm inside of her, I won't believe she's mine.

Her fingers make quick work of my buckle and fly, spreading my pants open to slip her hands inside to palm me. Biting back a moan, I toe off my shoes and shrug off my jacket while she unbuttons my shirt.

Naked and hard, I find a condom in the drawer. She steals the foil packet from me and opens it with her teeth, all the while staring into my eyes.

Objectively, Mae's a beautiful woman, but her beauty extends beyond her face and body. When I slide into her, her soul shines in her eyes, and I hope I'm worthy of her love.

Because now that I've had her, I don't think I'll ever be able to walk away. The thought of losing her stabs me deep in my chest, hitching my breath in my lungs.

Last night, sex with her was urgent and desperate. Tonight, I claim her with slow strokes and lingering kisses, drawing out her pleasure and pulling back right before she comes, teasing her until she begs and pleads for the touch that will send her over the edge. Once she has her second orgasm, I shift our position so I'm behind her, taking her with long, deep thrusts that force me to close my eyes as my own orgasm hits the point of no return. My hips jerk right before I come in a rush of blinding pleasure, leaving me panting and spent.

If she gives me the chance, I'll prove I'm worth her heart and all of her tomorrows.

<hr />

"Why do you have an alarm set for the middle of the night?" she murmurs against my chest.

"It's early morning and we need to get up." I kiss the top of her head and then sweep her hair from my chest and her face.

"There's nothing worth getting up for this early on a Sunday." She burrows farther under the covers.

"Some things are." I give her ass a squeeze.

"We can have sex again when it's light out."

"True, but we need to get dressed for the romantic gesture I promised you yesterday."

Rolling away from me, she opens one eye and peers at me in doubt.

"Come on." I lead by example and get out of bed.

"Standing around naked with a hard-on isn't working in your favor if you want to encourage me to leave this bed and apartment." She licks her bottom lip.

It would be so easy to step closer to her and slide my dick between her lips, but this morning is more than getting a blow job. We have later for that.

Minutes later, a sleepy Mae follows me through the garage

to my car. I give her a kiss and then open the door for her to climb inside.

Buckling her seatbelt, she arches an eyebrow. "Will all your romantic gestures require me to lose sleep?"

"Not all of them." I kiss her again before closing the door.

"Where are we going?" she asks, yawning.

"Not far." I drive in the direction of the club.

Less than five minutes later, I park the 4Runner in a spot in the mostly empty parking lot near the golf course.

My surprise sits a few yards away and can't be missed.

Mae presses her hand against her window. Her dark eyes are wide with shock and excitement when she twists to face me. "This is one helluva gesture."

"Go big or go home." I shrug, pretending I'm not as excited as she is. "Let's go."

The roar of the gas flame inflating the giant, balloon greets us outside of the car.

"Is this the same one Topher and Twyla were supposed to use today?" she asks, tilting her head back to stare at the huge, glowing, rainbow balloon sitting on the golf course.

"Figured they weren't going to be needing it and it's already paid for." Draping my arm over her shoulders, I pull her closer.

Mouth hanging open, she gapes at me and then back at the balloon.

"Is this okay?" I ask, suddenly doubting my idea.

"You've just ruined me for all other men. Are you okay with that? Because if this doesn't work out, I'm going to die alone with dozens of cats and a huge collection of balloon knick-knacks, and it will be all your fault." She gives me a sharp look that makes me laugh instead of cower.

"I'm more than okay with this idea." I kiss her once and then twice.

"Then I'm ready. Bring it on." Throwing her arms around

my neck, she kisses me back.

We're still on the ground, but she makes me feel like I'm soaring.

EPILOGUE

MAE

"WE SHOULD DITCH work and spend the day on the mountain." He kisses my neck and trails his fingers down my arm, sending goose bumps over my skin.

"We?" I ask, squirming on his lap. "You don't have a job to skip."

He stills my movement and then lifts his hips, rubbing his growing hard-on against my bottom. "True. Didn't you mention a sore throat earlier today? Headache? Isn't there a twenty-four hour stomach bug going around?"

I love that he's adapted my habit of coming up with hypothetical excuses to get out of things we don't want to do. "Last Sunday we both woke up with the stomach bug to avoid dinner with your parents. I don't want to jinx myself by using that one too frequently."

Post wedding scandal, we've had dinner with the Roberts at least once a week. I think Gwendolyn is still in denial over Landon because she never brings him up. Out of sight, out of mind. Easy to do when he and Twyla refuse to return to Aspen. They even skipped the holidays, which is the best possible decision they've made so far. At least they have some common sense when it comes to waiting for things to blow over before coming home. I imagine them on the run, constantly moving from place to place, but the reality is they're living together in a condo in Denver.

Topher moved to New York City, and if the local gossip has it right, is dating a lovely woman from Connecticut.

Aiden nuzzles my neck with his nose. "If the snow is deep enough, you'll have to work from home. For safety reasons."

"Oh, that one would be perfect."

"You're welcome." He pulls down the collar of my sweater to kiss my collarbone.

As the official Social Media Director for the Aspen Coalition, I'm working full time in the office. No more slinging crepes at La Belle Femme. I started the job in January after the huge success of the gala. Doesn't hurt my boyfriend is the newest board member and made a sizable donation to fund more staff. I have no issues with a little nepotism if it's for the greater good.

I'm thrilled with the position except it puts a dent in my time on the mountain. And it means I spend my days in the office instead of lounging around in bed all day with the afore-mentioned boyfriend.

We spend the time apart sending each other ridiculous text messages filled with random emojis we try to make dirty.

The end of ski season is a few weeks away and I'm looking forward to the silliness of Schneetag with the girls.

Rumor has it Lee is will be proposing to Sage, which is about damn time. Jesse was the first to start the trend over New Year's, with a sweet proposal involving his dog, Fern, wearing the engagement ring on her collar. Only took Mara two days to notice it. If Justin drops to one knee and asks Zoe to marry him, I'll once again be the odd girl out.

And I'm fine with that.

Because I know when Aiden proposes, it will be with the

most epic romantic gesture yet that will make me ugly cry.

Of course I'll say yes.

He's my person, my future, and my forever.

A NOTE FROM DAISY

THANK YOU FOR reading *Up to You*.

I hope you enjoyed Mae and Aiden's story. When I launched the Love with Altitude series, I said it would be four books long. Does that mean there won't be more books set in Aspen and Snowmass? Never say never.

I appreciate you taking the time to write an honest review and sharing it on Goodreads or your favorite retailer. Reviews and word of mouth are the best ways to spread the word about books we enjoy.

To keep up with my latest news and upcoming releases, sing up for my mailing list.

xo
Daisy

ABOUT DAISY

DAISY CURRENTLY LIVES in a real life Stars Hollow in the Boston suburbs with her husband, their rescue dog Mulder, and an indeterminate number of imaginary house goats. When not writing, she can be found in the garden, traveling to satiate her wanderlust, lost in a good book, or on social media, usually talking about books, bearded men, and sloths.

www.daisyprescott.com

www.twitter.com/Daisy_Prescott

www.facebook.com/daisyprescottauthorpage

www.instagram.com/daisyprescott

ACKNOWLEDGMENTS

TO MY HUSBAND, I couldn't do this without you. When I'm on deadline, hangry, over-caffeinated, sleep deprived, unwashed, snarling/crying/laughing as I write, you're there to support me. Whether it's with beta feedback, hashing out a sticky point in the plot, or gentle prodding to shower and eat, you're the reason I'm able to write "the end" on my books. Thank you for being my HEA.

Thank you to Shannon Lumetta for all of beautiful covers for this series. You're a magical sorceress. MJ, thanks for the early feedback and reminding me I can be funny.

I'm blessed to have an amazing team of editors and proof-readers: Melissa Ringsted at There for You Editing, Janice Owens, and Elli Reid. Grazie mille to Fiona for formatting this series. You are patient, kind, and the best cat herder around. To Jenn Beach, you are amazing. Thank you for all that you do behind the scenes and all of your insights. You keep my crazy train running smoothly.

Thank you to Jessica Estep and KP Simmon at Inkslinger PR for insight and guidance in all things marketing and promotion. Meire Dias at Bookcase Literary Agency, thank you for your ongoing championing of my books.

To the members of Daisyland, thanks for your enthusiasm and passion for my books. I love our virtual club house, To the RC, you're the wind beneath my wings. Thank you for your time and encouragement.

Thanks to my fellow authors who continue to inspire and encourage me. To Julie, Tina, and Melulia, thank you for cheering me on when I kept swearing this book would never be finished. To my fellow authors of the Nerdy Little Book Herd, thanks for all the laughs and being awesome. To the authors of the Cocky Collective, I'm proud to stand alongside. To the Indie book community, thank you for the years of support, friendship, wisdom, and generosity that goes beyond writing and publishing. To every blogger who shares, reads, reviews, and promotes the authors and books you love, thank you. We are a sisterhood.

Most of all, dear reader, thank you for reading this book. I appreciate every review, message, and email from you.

Hearing from my readers is the best part of publishing. I can be reached on social media or at *daisyauthor@gmail.com*.

xo

Daisy